Wife. The word hit Sam like a fist in the chest.

His throat had gone dry when Faith had walked into the judge's chambers a few minutes ago, wearing traditional white. He assumed her color choice was to convince everyone she truly was happy to be a bride. And whether their wedding guests believed this was a real marriage or not, they seemed determined to treat it as one.

Too bad Faith didn't feel the same way about the wedding night, Sam thought. The fact that he'd be sleeping alone tonight only increased his frustration. He had images of slipping that pretty dress off his bride's soft shoulders and making that slender, curvy body of hers lose control, wanting him as badly as he wanted her.

The cad in him wouldn't mind if she had a little too much to drink and fell into his arms, Sam thought, but his pride—and his honor—wanted her willing.

Wrangler Dads
1. *Madeleine's Cowboy*
Kristine Rolofson
2. *Cowboy's Kin*
Victoria Pade
3. *Trouble at Lone Spur*
Roz Denny Fox
4. *Upon a Midnight Clear*
Lynn Erickson
5. *Cowboy at the Wedding*
Karen Rose Smith
6. *Dangerous*
Caroline Cross
Reunion Western-Style!
7. *Rodeo Rider*
Stella Bagwell
8. *Mustang Valley*
Jackie Merritt
9. *Holding on to Alex*
Margaret Way
10. *Home Fires Burning Bright*
Laurie Paige
11. *One More Rodeo*
Lynnette Kent
12. *The Reckoning*
Joleen Daniels
Conveniently Wed
13. *Seduction of the Reluctant Bride*
Barbara McCauley
14. *Temporary Husband*
Day Leclaire
15. *The Wilde Bunch*
Barbara Boswell
16. *Her Torrid Temporary Marriage*
Sara Orwig
17. *The Newlywed Game*
Bonnie K. Winn
18. *Gideon's Bride*
Amelia Autin
Holding Out for a Hero
19. *Midnight Prey*
Caroline Burnes
20. *Bulletproof Heart*
Sheryl Lynn
21. *Hiding Out at the Circle C*
Jill Shalvis
22. *Lucky Devil*
Patricia Rosemoor
23. *She Caught the Sheriff*
Anne Marie Duquette
24. *The Unlikely Bodyguard*
Amy J. Fetzer

Rawhide & Lace
25. *Cowboys Are for Loving*
Marie Ferrarella
26. *The Rancher and the Redhead*
Allison Leigh
27. *White Gold*
Curtiss Ann Matlock
28. *Texas Dawn*
Joan Elliott Pickart
29. *Rancher's Choice*
Kylie Brant
30. *Delightful Jones*
Patricia Knoll
Kids & Kin
31. *The Troublemaker Bride*
Leanne Banks
32. *Cowboys Do It Best*
Eileen Wilks
33. *The Rancher and the Baby*
Elizabeth August
34. *Boss Lady and the Hired Hand*
Barbara McMahon
35. *The Cowboy's Courtship*
Patricia Thayer
36. *The Farmer Takes a Wife*
Jodi O'Donnell
Men of the Land
37. *The Badlands Bride*
Rebecca Winters
38. *The Cowboy Wants a Wife!*
Susan Fox
39. *Woman at Willagong Creek*
Jessica Hart
40. *Wyoming Wife?*
Shawna Delacorte
41. *Cowboys, Babies and Shotgun Vows*
Shirley Rogers
42. *Home Is Where Hank Is*
Martha Shields
Secrets!
43. *The Rancher's Runaway Bride*
Judith Bowen
44. *Midnight Cowboy*
Adrianne Lee
45. *Remember Me, Cowboy*
Caroline Burnes
46. *The Other Laura*
Sheryl Lynn
47. *A Man without Love*
Beverly Bird
48. *The Return of the Cowboy*
Cheryl Biggs

SEDUCTION OF THE RELUCTANT BRIDE

Barbara McCauley

CONVENIENTLY
Wed

Silhouette® Books
Published by Silhouette Books
America's Publisher of Contemporary Romance

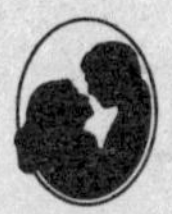

SILHOUETTE BOOKS

ISBN 0-373-65322-0

SEDUCTION OF THE RELUCTANT BRIDE

This edition published by arrangement with Harlequin Books S.A.

Visit Silhouette Books at www.eHarlequin.com

Printed in U.S.A.

BARBARA McCAULEY

Barbara McCauley has written more than twenty novels for Silhouette Books, and lives in Southern California with her own handsome hero husband, Frank, who makes it easy to believe in and write about the magic of romance. Barbara's stories have won and been nominated for numerous awards, including the prestigious RITA® Award from the Romance Writers of America, Best Desire of the Year from *Romantic Times* and Best Short Contemporary from the National Reader's Choice Awards.

Please address questions and book requests to:
Silhouette Reader Service
U.S.: 3010 Walden Ave., P.O. Box 1325, Buffalo, NY 14269
Canadian: P.O. Box 609, Fort Erie, Ont. L2A 5X3

To women everywhere
who've learned to listen with their hearts.

One

Digger Jones was dead.

No one in the town of Cactus Flat, Texas, could believe it, of course. Who ever would have thought a freak mountain storm would get the best of the crusty old café owner? He'd worked his mine in Lonesome Rock Canyon for more than forty years and survived broken bones, pneumonia, snake bite and weather that would have immobilized the city of New York. Digger Jones was too damn ornery to die.

But facts were facts. The storm had turned the canyon where Digger had camped into a raging river, washing out everything in its path. Search parties had turned up little more than half a tent and a few assorted articles of clothing. It might take months to find a body in the devastation the flood had left behind. More than likely, no body would be found.

With that thought in mind, Sam McCants frowned at the rose-covered coffin resting on the altar. There'd been no official declaration of death from the State, and Sam had argued with Hollis Fitcher, the town mortician, at the absurdity of a coffin without a body. Still, Hollis had insisted piously that Digger had paid in advance, in full, for the deluxe package that included the top-of-the-line oak casket. Body or not, the mortician had sniffed, Digger would have what he paid for.

The organist, also part of the deluxe package, broke into a lively rendition of *Amazing Grace,* signaling that the service would begin in a few minutes. Except for the last two rows, every pew in the small church was nearly filled. Digger might have been a cranky, cantankerous coffee shop owner and silver miner, but the entire town of Cactus Flat would miss him terribly.

Sam slipped into the front pew beside Jake Stone. Savannah, Jake's wife, looking beautifully slim after the birth of their second child, leaned over and kissed Sam's cheek. Sam winked playfully at the honey blonde.

Never mind that Jake and Sam had been best friends most of their lives, instinct—and Sam's notorious bachelor status—had Jake slipping an arm around Savannah anyway. ''Find your own woman, McCants.''

''Sam doesn't have to find women, dear. They find him.'' Savannah pressed a reassuring hand into her husband's and squeezed. ''Matilda tells me that just last week when Sam came into the Hungry Bear her business practically doubled—all female. She said there was a near brawl at Sam's booth when Pattie Wright tried to shove Marie Farrel out of her seat."

"Pattie slipped," Sam defended the pretty brunette. Small towns were a curse on a single man. Every move he made, every word he spoke to a female—any female—was like gasoline on the gossip fire. And definitely exaggerated. "We're just friends, that's all."

"And a man can never have too many friends, right?" Jake wiggled his eyebrows. When Savannah frowned at him, he cleared his throat. "So, we heard you were giving the eulogy."

Sam admired Jake's wisdom to change the subject. "Since Digger left me executor of his estate, Reverend Winslow thought I might like to say a few words."

"And what estate might that be?"

They all looked up as Jared, Jake's brother, slid into the pew behind them. Jared brushed Savannah's cheek with a brotherly kiss. "Other than a stuffed grizzly bear and a set of frying pans, Digger Jones didn't even own a watch."

"He loved that bear." Sam grinned at Jared. "I'm thinking about buying it myself and passing it along to you and Annie for the entryway of that new house you built. And speaking of your lovely wife, tell me she finally dumped you and the path is clear for me."

Had he been any other man but Sam McCants Jared would have had to hit him. Instead, he smiled good-naturedly. "The only clear path around Annie these days would be a 747 runway. Her due date is only two weeks away. Ah, here's the little woman now."

"I heard that crack." Annie slowly eased herself

down beside her husband, then coolly accepted his repentant kiss. "If I wouldn't have to fight my way through the long line of women, I just might take Sam up on his offer. At least he knows how to treat a lady."

The third Stone sibling, Jessica Stone Grant, slid into the pew beside Annie. "He knows how to treat a lady, all right. *All* the ladies. Don't look now, Sam, but Carol Sue Gibson is sitting with Sarah Pearson and they're both looking moon-eyed at you."

Two delightful specimens of the female gender, Sam thought as he turned and grinned at the women. Carol Sue crossed her legs, hiking up her skirt and Sarah licked her glossy red lips.

Ah, it's good to be alive.

"*Friends,* I'm telling you. We're just friends," he said casually and settled back in his seat.

Jessica, Annie and Savannah rolled their eyes, while Jared and Jake exchanged a knowing smirk.

Jessica leaned forward and whispered in Sam's ear. "Watch out, sweetheart, one day one of your 'friends' is going to have you on your knees."

Jared and Jake were shaking their heads as Dylan, Jessica's husband, slid into the pew beside her. "You want to explain to me why you're whispering in another man's ear before, or after, I slug him?"

Jessica gave Dylan a peck on his lips, then wiped a smudge of baby food off his cheek. "It's just Sam, darling. You get Daniel off all right at Josephine's?"

"Soon as our son saw his cousins were there, too, I might as well have been the mailman. See what you have to look forward to, Sam?" Dylan slipped an arm around his wife and she automatically leaned into him. "Baby food and babysitters."

The intimate look they exchanged, Sam noted, relayed there was plenty more to their marriage. "That's the Stone family department," Sam said with the assured confidence of a confirmed bachelor. "Preachers and promises are not in this boy's future."

The organist punctuated Sam's words with a deep rumbling chord, heavy with foreboding. An odd sensation scooted up Sam's spine, and he shifted restlessly in his seat.

Then, as suddenly as the organist had intensified her playing, she hesitated and stumbled. The buzz in the church seemed to quiet, as well. Baffled, Sam glanced over his shoulder. All heads turned toward the entrance at the back of the church.

A young woman stood in the shadows of the foyer, with the sun at her back. Afternoon light danced off her shoulder-length golden blond hair. She wore black, a double-breasted suit that emphasized her small waist and revealed long, long legs encased in black silk and high heels. A small purse dangled from a gold chain off one smooth shoulder, hugging the curve of her slender hip. She stood there, motionless, her cool gaze resting on the rose-covered coffin, then glanced casually around the church.

Every man straightened, every woman stiffened. Sam simply couldn't breathe.

She was a stranger, no question of that. Sam had lived and ranched in Stone Creek County outside of Cactus Flat his entire life. He knew everyone who lived here and most everyone in the surrounding counties, too. This woman wasn't from anywhere around here. She was city, with a capital *C*.

What the hell was she doing here, at Digger Jones's funeral?

"Goodness," Jessica breathed.

Not exactly the first word that had come to Sam's mind, but a close derivative, he thought. There were other words, too. Cool. Sophisticated. Chic. Untouchable. He watched her scan the pews with thickly lashed eyes, and from across the room he wondered about their color. It surprised him how much he suddenly wanted an answer to that question.

The organist found her beat in the music again and Reverend Winslow, who had also paused to stare curiously at the stranger, took his place at the pulpit.

The woman moved to the last row and sat, her back straight, her unblinking gaze focused solely on the Reverend. The music stopped, then reluctantly bodies shifted and heads turned back to the front of the church.

Reverend Winslow straightened his shoulders and cast a long, imperious glance over the room, pausing momentarily at the last pew. Sam grinned at the thought of the pious Reverend Winslow caught under the blond stranger's spell, but even men of the cloth were allowed fantasies, weren't they?

And this woman was definitely the stuff fantasies were made out of. He could have sworn he saw lace poking out from under her suit jacket. Black lace against creamy white skin. What man wouldn't wonder what was under that cool exterior, if those silky black stockings went all the way up those long legs to that narrow waist, or if they cut off at her thighs, thighs that…

Jake elbowed him.

"Huh?" Coming out of his daydream, it was the most intelligent response he could manage. Jake nodded toward the pulpit. Reverend Winslow had obviously already introduced him and now stared disapprovingly down at him.

Damn.

He tamped down the rush of blood to his brain, stood, then straightened his jacket and made his way to the pulpit.

Joseph Alexander Courtland III had instructed his only daughter at a very young age on the importance of disciplined emotion. For that, especially at this moment, Faith was extremely grateful.

She'd seen all the heads turn when she'd walked into the small church. Felt their curious stares and wary glances. Strangers were not to be trusted, she understood. But then, Faith thought dryly, quite often, neither were friends or family.

The minister, dressed in a flowing black robe, had thinning brown hair and wore round, wire-framed glasses. His solemn voice welcomed everyone, then he glanced at her and introduced himself as Reverend Winslow. Since everyone else in the church obviously knew the Reverend, Faith realized with dread that the man was speaking directly to her. Resisting the urge to squirm, Faith simply stared back, pretending not to notice that several heads had turned discreetly her way.

The Reverend quoted several comforting psalms,

spoke briefly of the tragic loss of Francis Elijah Montgomery, better known as Digger Jones to the town of Cactus Flat, then called on one of Digger's friends to speak. Faith froze at the introduction.

Sam McCants.

A man rose from the front pew where he'd been seated. The man she'd come here to see. She'd expected someone older. Digger had been seventy-two. Faith had assumed the man that he had appointed as executor for his estate would be a peer, a life-long friend. Someone closer to his own age. This man couldn't be more than thirty-four or -five.

He was certainly tall, she thought, watching him walk smoothly to the pulpit. At least six-two, maybe even six-three. His thick, wavy hair touched the collar of his white dress shirt and was almost as black as the tailored suit he wore. A suit, Faith noted with interest, that fit his broad shoulders and narrow waist like a glove. Her gaze drifted just below the waist, and she felt a tug of curiosity, wondering if his suit jacket covered a backside that was as well-shaped as the rest of his muscular body.

The improper thought caught Faith completely off guard. Frowning, she straightened and carefully reined in her wayward wondering. She had a job to do here, she reminded herself sharply. The sooner she completed that job, the sooner she could be back in Boston. It was imperative she stay focused.

When the man turned and looked straight at her, her focus tumbled.

The face matched the body: dark, intense eyes; strong, masculine features; a jaw that advertising agencies paid big bucks for. Only when he looked away from her did she realize she'd been holding her breath.

"Digger Jones," the man said, his voice deep and resonant, "was the most irascible, ill-natured, argumentative, opinionated man I've met in my entire life."

She nearly gasped out loud. How could he say such a thing after a man had so tragically lost his life? Shocked, Faith glanced around the church. Everyone was nodding.

"And no one," Sam said, "no one, loved him more than me."

There were smiles now. Some of the ladies dabbed at their eyes. Relieved, Faith leaned back in the pew. Any resentment or grievance with Digger from Mr. McCants, or from the town, might complicate her business here.

"Many of you—" Sam said, moving to the coffin "—are probably thinking what I'm thinking. That this casket lid is going to fly open any minute, with Digger ranting and raving, wanting to know what all the fuss is about and why the hell isn't Matilda flipping burgers and frying potatoes at lunchtime?"

There were chuckles throughout the church and a loud nose-blow from a big-haired platinum blonde in the second pew. Matilda, Faith assumed.

"But we all know," he went on, "that this coffin is empty. Digger is still in the mountains. In the canyons that he loved, where he worked, his entire life. Some people may have thought him foolish, crazy even, to live his life chasing after a silver mine. But I admired him. His tenacity, his determination, his dream. His apple cobbler."

When Sam looked heavenward, laughter broke out and Faith pressed her lips tightly together. She'd only been to two other funerals in her life, the first one four years ago, when she was twenty-two. Randolph Hollingsworth, the founder of the Boston Businessmen's Association, had passed on at eighty-four. Dignity and formality had been protocol for the elderly gentleman. Even when Russel Matthews's toupee had slipped off his head and fell directly onto Widow Hollingsworth's lap no one had laughed.

And then there was her second funeral, only six months ago.

Her father's.

There'd certainly been no laughter there, either. The service for Joseph Alexander Courtland III had been solemn, the reception afterward hushed and reserved. Like the man himself.

"I was only ten the first time Digger took me into the mountains to mine with him," Sam continued, and Faith drew in a breath to refocus her attention. "I just knew I was going to come home rich, with silver nuggets bulging out of my pockets."

He paused and smiled at the coffin. "What I came back with was a sore butt from four days in the saddle and hands that had more blisters than Pete Johnson has teeth."

The crowd laughed again, and a pole-shaped man in a too-small suit rose, tipping his cowboy hat as he grinned at everyone with a smile reminiscent of a woodchuck.

"But a young boy's disappointment," Sam said quietly, "became a man's realization. A realization that I did come home rich from that trip, that I brought back much more with me than any amount of riches could ever buy. Digger taught me perseverance, to never give up on what I value most, no matter what the cost. To treasure our families, our goals, our dreams.''

Sam touched the coffin, a tender gesture of farewell. ''Goodbye, Digger Jones. You may never have found your treasure, but you were one of the richest men I've ever had the pleasure, and the honor, to know.''

The organist began to play as Sam walked back to his seat. Faith struggled to blink back the tears threatening to spill. What was the matter with her? She had no reason to cry. No reason at all, she told herself. She was tired from the trip, under tremendous pressure at the moment, nervous about meeting Mr. McCants.

So what if the man's eulogy was touching? So what if Digger had made such an impact on these people's lives? None of that had anything to do with her, or why she was here. She was Faith Alexis Courtland, daughter of Joseph Alexander Courtland III and Colleen Jane Buchanan. She did not cry at funerals, and she most certainly did not laugh.

One by one, the townspeople passed by the coffin, men with their hats in their hands, women dabbing their eyes with tissues. Faith stayed where she was, ignoring the curious looks from the people of Cactus Flat as they filed out of the church.

To keep her eyes diverted and her hands busy, she fumbled in her purse for a tissue. She had no desire to talk with anyone, and she waited until the church was nearly empty before she tucked her tissue back into her purse. A few deep breaths and she would be fine. In control. Composed.

"Is there something I can help you with?"

Faith snapped her head around and stared into Sam McCants's dark eyes. She stood quickly, too quickly, and her purse slipped from her fingers, still unclasped. The contents skittered over the worn, but shiny oak floor.

Great—just great, Faith thought with a silent groan. A terrific first impression.

Her eyes were blue, Sam noted. The color of pale, soft denim. He'd caught her off guard, he realized, and for just a moment, before she'd straightened her shoulders and lifted that cute little chin, he'd seen something in those wide eyes that belied her outer image of cool sophistication. A distress that went deeper than a spilled purse.

He bent to help her, but they moved at the same time and only managed to bump into each other. The contact, though only a fraction of a second, brought forth an image of heated flesh. The sudden flush on her high cheeks charmed him. He caught her scent. Expensive. Exotic.

She stepped back, the windows in her eyes closed now. "Excuse me."

Her formality amused him as much as it intrigued him. He watched her bend demurely and scoop up a slim black wallet, palm-size brush and set of keys with a rental car insignia. He enjoyed the extra inches of exposed leg as she reached for a gold-toned ballpoint pen.

"Do you mind?" she asked.

He thought he'd been caught sneaking a peek, but

she was gesturing to the silver-cased lipstick that had rolled between his feet. He bent to pick it up, glancing at the label as he handed it to her. "Passion's Blush," he read aloud. "Very nice."

She dropped the silver tube into her purse, snapped the purse shut and adjusted the gold chain over her shoulder as she stood. "Faith Courtland, Mr. McCants."

He looked down at the hand she extended to him. Her tone was as stiff as the starched collars his mother had made him wear to Sunday school when he was a boy. "We're laid back here in Cactus Flat, Faith. Why don't you just call me Sam?"

She nodded, then smiled hesitantly. "Sam."

Her fingers were long and smooth. Warm. And no rings. He held her hand longer than he should have. "I've never seen you before, Faith." He would definitely have remembered. "Are you a friend of Digger's?"

"Digger?" she repeated. She cleared her throat, then tugged her hand from his. "Oh, yes, of course. Mr. Montgomery. No, I'm not a friend. Actually, Mr. McCants, I mean Sam, I'm here to see you."

It took a moment for her words to sink in, another longer moment for them to register. Of all the things he might have expected her to say, that was the last. "You're here to see *me?*"

"You *are* the man that Mr. Montgomery appointed as executor of his estate, aren't you? Owner of the Circle B ranch in Stone Creek County?"

How would she know that? And why did she keep referring to *Mr. Montgomery?* Digger had a tendency to punch anyone who called him by his real name.

"Yes," he answered slowly. "Digger did appoint me executor. But I doubt that you're interested in a stuffed grizzly bear or set of frying pans."

"Pardon me?"

"Never mind. I have a reception to go to over at the hotel. You're welcome to join me, but why don't we just get whatever it is you came here to say out of the way first."

"Yes, of course." She cleared her throat. "Mr. McCants—Sam—I'd like to inform you that I—we—at Elijah Jane Corporation are most anxious to work with you toward settling the matter of Mr. Mont—Digger's—holdings."

"Elijah Jane Corporation? As in the restaurant chain?" Sam frowned. "Why would they be interested in Digger? And what holdings are you talking about? Digger ran a small diner here in town, in a rented space, and lived in a tiny apartment at the hotel. He had an old truck, at least he had one until six months ago when Andy over at the gas station gave it last rites. That, other than the grizzly bear and frying pans I already mentioned, are the extent of Digger's holdings."

Her incredible blue eyes widened. "You mean, you don't know?"

Her startled question, sort of a throaty whisper, skimmed over him like silky fingers. "Know what?"

Her composure was back now, her face controlled and voice steady. "Mr. McCants, Francis Elijah Montgomery, known to you as Digger Jones, was the sole owner of Elijah Jane Corporation, a company with gross sales of over two-hundred-million dollars and a net worth of approximately twenty-million dollars."

Two

Faith watched Sam's face go blank as he stared at her. His eyes, filled with impatience only a moment ago, were empty now, void of any emotion.

Then he began to laugh.

It started off as a low rumble in his broad chest, then spread to a rolling wave of hilarity. He sat in the pew, shaking his head, and the sound of his laughter echoed in the now empty church.

Faith had no idea how to respond to Sam's display of amusement. She'd negotiated million-dollar deals with the toughest clients in Boston and Colorado, calmed an entire room of excited stockholders, settled disputes between employees and management. Those things were all in a day's work. She thrived on it, flourished in the order and control she executed. And still, at this moment, she couldn't seem to manage one discomposed cowboy.

Why was this one man throwing off her equilibrium so badly?

Certainly not because he was handsome. She met handsome men all the time. Faith Courtland was not the type to be influenced by a pretty face. Sam McCants might have the darkest, most extraordinary eyes she'd ever seen, and maybe there was an aura of blatant sexuality she'd never encountered before. That cute shock of black hair falling over his forehead might even tempt a weaker woman. But not her. No way.

"Twenty...million...dollars," he managed between guffaws. "Oh, sweetheart, that's ripe. You're good, I gotta tell you. Real good. You almost had me there."

Almost had him? He still didn't believe her? Exasperated, she tucked her hair behind her ear and straightened. "Mr. McCants, let me assure you—"

Faith let out a small squeak as Sam grabbed her hand and pulled her down beside him. "Sweetheart, I'll let you do anything you like to me. Just tell me, was it Jared or Jake? Both, right? I don't know where they found you, but you're one sweet filly. Damn, those boys are good."

This was going all wrong. Every rehearsed statement, every carefully developed stage of her agenda here was being shot to hell. She had no idea what this man was talking about, and with his chest suddenly pressed up against her, pushing her back against the pew, she suddenly found it difficult to think at all.

She felt the heat of his body seep through her silk jacket and slide over her skin. His mouth hovered mere inches from hers, those sexy eyes of his half closed, barely revealing a mixture of amusement and desire.

"Mr. McCants, Sam, please."

His breath fanned her earlobe, then her cheek. "I love the way you say please," he murmured huskily. "Say it again."

She almost did, then stopped herself, pressing a hand to his chest and pushing him away. Heart pounding, she stood on shaky knees and tugged at her jacket.

"I don't know anyone named Jared or Jake," she said, embarrassed that her voice cracked. "And no one 'found me,' as you so crudely put it. I'm here as vice president of Elijah Jane Corporation, and whether you believe it or not, Digger Jones does—did—indeed own the company."

Her fingers were shaking as she reached inside her purse and pulled a business card from her wallet. Sam held his gaze on hers as he took the card.

"Elijah Jane Corporation," he read aloud. "Boston, Massachusetts. Faith Alexis Courtland, Vice President." He glanced back up at her. "So the Stone brothers didn't hire you to snooker me?"

Snooker? Faith wasn't sure what it meant, but she didn't like the sound of it one little bit. "A man's funeral is hardly the time to 'snooker' anyone, Mr. McCants. Elijah Jane Corporation is devastated over Mr. Montgomery's tragic accident."

She *was* serious, Sam realized, taking in the firm set of her upturned lips and the fixed look in her pretty eyes. Completely serious. This woman really believed what she was saying.

There was a mistake here, of course, Sam knew.

Some bizarre twist of fate had mysteriously mixed up Digger Jones of Cactus Flat with some other fellow, who just happened, by some weird coincidence, to have the same name: Francis Elijah Montgomery.

But bizarre or not, who was he to question fate? She'd find out soon enough she had the wrong man. He just hoped it wouldn't be *too* soon. This time of the year was slow at the ranch. A little diversion—especially one with bottomless blue eyes and enticing curves—would be more than welcome.

Faith snapped her purse shut and tossed back her neatly trimmed, shoulder-length blond hair. "In case you haven't heard of us, we have fifty restaurants across the country, plus an extensive frozen food line carried by most grocery stores. We're famous for our steaks and ribs," she said proudly.

Sam might have mentioned to Faith that he had a freezer full of Elijah Jane's Hearty Homestyle Meals for the nights that Gazella, his housekeeper, had off, but that clipped, cool tone had crept back into her voice and he wouldn't give Miss Faith Courtland, *Vice President,* the satisfaction. And he wondered what she might say if he told her that he supplied the beef, through a distributor, for those steaks Elijah Jane was so famous for.

He pocketed her business card, then settled his arms over the back of the pew as he looked up at her. Damn, but this woman was easy on the eyes...and hard on the hormones. "I believe I've heard the name before, once or twice."

He was making fun of her, Faith was certain of it. But in spite of herself, and as hard as she wanted to be offended, she found the glint of humor in his eyes fascinating, and much to her distress, extremely appealing.

"Mr. McCants—" she began, clearing her throat "—Mr. Montgomery, Digger, has always been reclusive. A mystery owner who preferred to stay in the shadows and let his carefully selected employees run his company. His only demands were the highest quality food, absolute best service, and detailed weekly reports."

He watched her for a long moment, his arms draped casually over the pew, a mixture of interest and disbelief in his eyes. She resisted the urge to look away from his penetrating gaze.

"So you're telling me," he said finally, "that you've never even met this guy, your boss. Never even seen him."

She glanced at the front of the church, at the empty coffin, her chest tightening at the realization she never would. "That's right."

"How did you communicate?"

"There was a post office box in Midland, but the majority of communication was by computer and fax."

"Computer? Fax?" Sam gave a bark of laughter. "Digger didn't even own a cash register at the café. Said they were too much trouble. Sorry, sweetheart, but you've got the wrong man. You should have called and saved yourself a trip."

She blew out her irritation, then drew in a slow, calming breath. "Mr. Montgomery left your name and address only, with instructions to contact you at the Circle B if anything happened to him. It wasn't uncommon not to hear from him for a few weeks, but after a month, we contacted the local authorities here and found out that Francis Elijah Montgomery, alias Digger Jones, had been lost in the mountains after a flood. As vice president of Elijah Jane, it's my responsibility to meet with you and Mr. Montgomery's attorney to go over the details of his will and estate.''

Sam snorted. ''An attorney? Digger? I wouldn't even repeat his opinion of lawyers to a lady. 'Course, I wouldn't repeat most of Digger's opinions to a lady.''

''No lawyer?'' She frowned. ''But that's impossible. He must have had a lawyer draw up a will.''

Sam shook his head. '''Fraid not. Digger drew up his own a few months back, sealed it and gave it to me to handle for him when the time came. The bank's closed on Saturday, but we can check it out Monday morning. Until then, it's safe and sound in my safe deposit vault.''

Jaw slack, all she could do was stare at him. ''He drew up his own will and just handed it over to you, without any legal advice or representation?''

Annoyance flashed quickly in his eyes, the humor gone now. ''This isn't Boston, Ms. Courtland. Folks trust each other here.''

She hadn't meant to insult him, it was just so...so preposterous. ''Twenty-million dollars is a lot of trust by anyone's standards, in any city. A man doesn't just scribble away that kind of money in a hand-written will.''

''You didn't know Digger very well, did you?'' Sam said, his tone mocking.

''I told you, I never met the man.'' She let the burn

of his words pass, then lifted her chin. "But then, it appears that you didn't know him so well yourself."

"Perhaps." He stood, regarded her carefully. "I'd say, Ms. Courtland, under the circumstances, that we both have a lot to learn."

The reception for Digger was held in the banquet room of the Cactus Flat Hotel. Tables stretched from one end of the Spanish-style hall to the other; baskets and plates and pots filled with food had been supplied by the local ladies. The smell of fried chicken, barbecued ribs and Hattie Lamotts's honeyed ham filled the air. Chocolate cakes, warm cookies and frosted brownies enticed even those with the strongest willpower to give in. Food was a means of bringing people together, whether sharing conversation, joy or tragedy. It fed the stomach, and the soul as well.

Sam watched Faith nibble on one of Savannah Stone's Georgia-spiced chicken wings and decided it also fed another equally important aspect of the human species.

Lust.

Her perfectly straight, perfectly white teeth nipped delicately at the seasoned meat, then she daintily licked her passion-pink lips with the tip of her tongue. Sam might have groaned out loud if Jared, Jake and Dylan hadn't been standing next to him, watching him like proverbial hawks since he'd walked into the hall with the glamorous Faith Courtland at his side. Annie, Savannah and Jessica had Faith surrounded at the moment, talking as if they'd known each other for years.

Sam had warned Faith that it might be better not

to discuss exactly who she was with anyone else, or why she'd come to Cactus Flat. He'd also suggested that when she was asked, as she most certainly would be, she simply explain she was the niece of one of Digger's old friends who'd been unable to attend. Faith had stiffened at his suggestion, in that prim little manner of hers, but had relented, agreeing that it might be best not to discuss Digger's financial situation, or the reason for her visit, just yet.

Sam still didn't believe it, of course. Digger Jones, owner of a multimillion-dollar company? Sure. Next thing he knew, Faith Courtland would be selling him beach-front in Abilene. Lord knows, he just might buy it, too. If she'd been in his arms one minute longer back there in the church, he'd have bought cow hats if she'd wanted him to.

He'd seen the flutter of her pulse at the base of her throat when he'd pulled her close, felt the sudden rise of heat from her smooth skin. And those soft, firm breasts pressed against his chest had him aching to the point of pain. He'd been close enough to kiss her—nearly had, in fact, until she'd pushed him away. And in spite of her indignant formality with him, he'd had the distinct feeling that she'd wanted him to kiss her.

Sam looked at her now, at her squared shoulders, her long, lovely neck held high with all the grace of royalty. It gave him extreme satisfaction to know that he'd rattled the cool Ms. Courtland's cage, if only for a moment. He'd have to work on stretching that moment out. Like, an entire night. Or two, he thought with a smile. She'd be stuck here at least until Monday morning, when he could prove to her Digger's "estate" consisted of little more than some restaurant equipment and mining supplies. Once she realized she'd made a mistake, she'd be on the next plane out of Midland Airport. A pity, he thought, his gaze skimming over the curve of her hips and long legs.

The ladies joined the men and Jake, almost as if he'd been reading Sam's mind, asked Faith how long she'd be staying.

She slid her baby-blue eyes in Sam's direction. "Actually, that depends on Sam. I wouldn't want to impose, but my…uncle, being an old friend of Digger's and unable to travel since his surgery, asked if I would take a few days and visit with those people who knew Digger well. He thought I might bring back a few stories."

A few days? Sam lifted a brow as he held Faith's gaze. She could be out of here before noon day after tomorrow. Why would she stay longer than that? Not that he minded, of course, but it just didn't make any sense. This woman was getting harder to read by the moment.

"Come for Sunday dinner tomorrow night," Savannah offered. "We've all got a story or two you can take back to your uncle. We're about as close to family as Digger ever had."

Though it was subtle, Sam noticed Faith's hesitation, the tightening of her body, the imperceptible narrowing of her eyes. She'd been caught in her own web of fabrication, Sam thought, and that pristine sense of propriety of hers refused to let her turn down Savannah's invitation. She had gotten herself into it, he thought with annoyance. He had no intention of bailing her out. More than likely, she was already imagining an evening that would be more boring than watching a tree grow.

Still, as she thanked Savannah, Sam heard a slight tremble in Faith's voice that had him wondering.

"Couldn't help but overhear you were looking to talk to some of Digger's friends." Irv Meyers, the deputy sheriff, strutted into the tight circle. "Digger and me were best buddies."

Best buddies, my eye.

Sam frowned at the owl-faced man. "Was that before or after Digger chased you down the street with a baseball bat?" he asked.

Irv tugged defensively at the belt circling his thick waist. "I warned him plenty before I gave him that parking ticket. Digger knew that. He never held a grudge."

Everyone laughed at that, causing Irv's face to redden. Anyone who knew Digger at all, knew damn well he hadn't spoken to Irv in two years.

"Thank you, Deputy Meyers." Faith held out her hand and Irv nearly tripped over his feet as he took it. "I'll be sure to call you."

The list of Digger's "best buddies" kept growing, much to Sam's annoyance. With the word out—and the word did travel fast—that Faith wanted to talk to people about Digger, every unmarried male in town, not to mention a few married ones, suddenly had a story.

Sam was about to step in and break up the crowd when he felt a hand on his arm. Carol Sue, with her fiery red hair and seductive smile, held out a slice of chocolate cake.

"Thought you might like some sweets," she said

with a throaty whisper, batting her big green eyes at him, suggesting she was offering more than cake.

With a smile that came to Sam as automatically as a heartbeat, he took the cake and sniffed at it. "Umm. You always been a mind reader, Carol Sue?"

Her lips curved upward slowly, like a cat who'd just spied a mouse. "I bet I could guess what you're thinking right now," she purred.

He hoped not. Sam knew if the redhead had even an inkling that while he was accepting cake from her he was thinking about Faith Courtland's luscious lips, he'd be washing chocolate frosting out of his hair for a week. "My thoughts might shock you, darling," Sam said with a wicked grin.

"Why don't you call me later and we'll see who shocks whom." She walked away, waggling her fingers. When Sam turned back to the circle of men who'd surrounded Faith, he noticed she was gone.

Frowning, he set about looking for her in the hall—casually, of course—but she was nowhere to be seen. He strolled nonchalantly to the lobby of the hotel, wondering if she'd gone to the ladies' room, when he spotted her sitting by herself outside in the covered courtyard.

She looked small in the oversized wicker chair. Her shoulders were hunched slightly forward, her eyes cast downward, her expression one of absolute despair. He had no idea what had prompted her sudden melancholy, but it appeared that she wanted to be left alone.

As he continued to watch her, despite his good sense and scruples, he couldn't shake the lure of her vulnerability. There were two women here: one cool and distant, in control; the other crestfallen and weary. Both of them were extremely appealing.

The sadness in her eyes drew him to her. He sat beside her, and she immediately stiffened. He could see her struggle to compose herself. It was a battle hard-won.

"Tired?"

She started to shake her head, then smiled softly. "Maybe a little."

He gave her a sly, half grin. "I've got just the thing."

Her expression was guarded now, but curious. "And that is?"

"Chocolate."

He leaned close, stabbing a big bite of cake along with a healthy dose of frosting and holding it to her lips. She eyed it like a penniless child outside a candy store, then put up a hand and shook her head.

He waved it under her nose, watched her stiff shoulders melt as she breathed in the exquisite fragrance. Her eyes closed halfway, as if she were floating on a sea of physical delight.

He'd only meant to comfort her, ease whatever mood had overcome her. But now, as he watched her willpower succumb to the rich scent of the chocolate, he knew he wanted this woman, wanted her under him, with that same expression, his name on her lips, her hands on his skin.

And when she gave in and opened her lips for a taste, then moaned softly, he thought he just might drop to his knees right there.

"Sinful," she whispered, her voice filled with an ecstasy that had Sam grinding his back teeth.

He wanted to taste her—taste the chocolate mingling with her own warm, sensuous flavor—with a desperation that nearly brought a sweat to his brow. He eased back, shocked by the force of the need ripping through him, and angry with himself that just when he'd finally gotten this woman to let down her guard, if only a little, all he could think of was getting her into his bed.

"Sam." She'd closed her eyes and the sound of his name, spoken so softly, rippled through him like a heatwave. "Can we go upstairs?"

This time he *did* break out in a sweat. Was she suggesting what he hoped she was suggesting? Damn. He would have brought the entire cake over if he'd known chocolate was the pass key.

"Uh, sure."

"Do you have the key?"

Why would he have the key to her room? "Don't you?"

She opened one eye, then the other and sat up straight. Her brow knotted as she stared at him. "Why would I have a key to Digger's room?"

Damn, damn, damn. That's what she meant. "Oh, right. I can, uh, get the key from Jerome, the desk clerk."

She watched him for a moment. "Did you think I was asking you up to my room?"

That cool tone was back now, the vulnerability and sadness gone; a fierce, accusatory look glinted in her eyes. "Mr. McCants, I'll have you know I'm an engaged woman. And even if I weren't, I don't invite strange men up to my room."

It was on the tip of his tongue to ask her if she

invited men she knew, but somehow he didn't think she'd appreciate the humor. Damn. Engaged.

But not married. He stood and offered her a hand. "Is the ring on a layaway plan?"

Ignoring him, she rose and brushed past him. "It's not quite official yet. Not that it's any of your business."

"Just making conversation." Grinning, he followed her. "So who's the lucky guy?"

She stopped and turned so abruptly he nearly ran into her. "Let's just get the room key and get this over with, all right?"

An elderly couple, Ed and Thelma Winters, walked by just then, and stared. Sam smiled at them and nodded. Faith blushed.

"Red's a lovely color on you, Faith," he whispered. "You should wear it more often."

With a groan, she turned on her heels and walked to the front desk. He followed, cursed his bad luck and Faith Courtland's not quite official fiancé, whoever the hell he was.

The two-room "suite," as the desk clerk had called it, was no bigger than a closet, Faith thought as Sam opened the door and she stepped inside. Late-afternoon sun peeked through the blinds into the dark, stuffy room. The faint aroma of old cigars lingered in the stale air.

"No one's been in here except Jerome since Digger disappeared." Sam flipped up the blinds and opened a window. Light poured into the room, illuminating dust motes that scattered as the breeze rushed in carrying the scent of honeysuckle vine. He turned back to her, brushing off his hands. "Hardly the residence of a multi-millionaire."

Yes, indeed, Faith agreed, glancing around. The furniture was sparse, nothing more than a simple blue couch and scarred coffee table, a fat easy chair, a large brown metal desk and mismatched chair. In the bedroom, a king-sized bed and small dresser. Simple was the only word to describe it.

She walked around, trying to imagine why he lived like this. He could have bought a villa in Spain. A chateau in France. An estate in Cape Cod. He could have lived anywhere he wanted, bought anything he wanted. Yet he chose to stay here in Cactus Flat, to work in a coffee shop, to mine for silver, and to live in a rented hotel room.

"You still think this is the same Digger Jones you're looking for?" Sam asked, watching her as she walked back into the living room. He'd pulled off his suit jacket, tugged off his tie, and settled his long, muscular frame in the easy chair, slinging both arms over the back.

The I-told-you-so look in his eyes annoyed her, but then she was still smarting from his believing that she'd suggested they go to bed together. And they'd just met, for heaven's sake!

The nerve of the man. The arrogance. So what if he was good-looking and had a certain…charm. That certainly didn't mean a woman was going to drop her knickers if he crooked a finger.

But there was that woman at the reception, that redhead who had fawned all over Sam, batting her eyelashes and leaning up against him. And that blonde who'd come up to Savannah and asked where

Sam was. She'd had a predatory look in her eyes, too. No wonder the man had a swelled head.

Forcing her mind back to the issue, Faith moved to the desk in the corner. Under a white tablecloth sat what appeared to be a computer—the only incongruous article in the modest room. She pulled the dusty cloth off the large monitor and turned to grin at Sam. "My, my. What have we here?"

The computer, and a monitor, were top-of-the-line, state-of-the-art equipment. A laser printer—color, no less—and also first-class, sat beside the computer. Sam's eyebrows lifted and the surprise in his eyes gave Faith a certain sense of satisfaction. "There's a fax, too," she said somewhat smugly. "Now what do you think an old silver miner would want with all this equipment?"

"Games?" Sam rose and moved closer, peering down at the computer as if it were an alien spaceship.

"War games, maybe." She pulled a pair of glasses out of her purse, slipped them on, then flipped on the computer and monitor. "This baby could launch a missile."

The computer hummed and the monitor flashed a soft amber light. She entered her password, then pulled up the file labeled EJCORP. Sam stood behind her, watching as she pulled up file after file, accounts with suppliers, stats on the eastern chain of restaurants, profit-and-loss statements on the division that handled the frozen food division.

"This is the main office," she explained, pulling up the Boston file. "Mr. Montgomery—Digger—had the entire company at his fingertips here." She laughed softly. "I'd always imagined a large, elegant office somewhere, surrounded by rich woods, lush carpeting and silver paperweights.''

Frowning, Sam picked up a baseball-sized chunk of granite sitting on top of several thick manila file folders and stared at it. ''Looks like he had a lot of people imagining wrong.''

She glanced up at him over her shoulder. She'd been so immersed in pulling up the files that she hadn't realized how close he'd moved in behind her, that one hand rested on the back of her chair, brushing her shoulder. She forced herself to ignore the jolt of heat that shot through her body. ''So you finally believe mc?''

He shrugged, setting the rock back on the desk. ''I'm not sure what I believe. I've known Digger Jones my entire life. As far back as I can remember he's been mining silver, frying burgers and grilling steaks. Nobody could cook like that man. He makes—made—an apple cobbler that made you want to cry, it was so good. The only other cobbler I ever had that even came close was at—''

He stopped and Faith twisted around to face him, her lips slowly turning up at the corners. They said it at the same time. ''Elijah Jane.''

Could it be? Digger Jones, hardened, crusty old miner and café owner, owner of a multimillion-dollar business?

Sam sat on the edge of the desk and dragged his hands through his hair. This was too incredible. Impossible. Sam looked up at Faith, who was watching him with a touch of amusement in her eyes. He thought her glasses made her look adorable.

''His apple cobbler was how it got started, actually.

Almost thirty years ago.'' She pressed one slender fingertip on a button and only the amber light remained on the screen. ''Rumor had it Digger had a cousin in Boston, Leo Jenuski, who wanted to open a sandwich shop in the business district. Leo talked Digger into loaning him the money, then skipped out three months after he opened his doors. It was either forget the money, or come in and make it successful himself. Within six months, the shop was packed from opening to closing, with customers arguing over Digger's apple cobbler.''

''Well, that much hasn't changed.'' He wondered if she had any idea how her eyes softened and voice deepened when she talked about Elijah Jane. Or how damn appealing he found it. ''There've been fistfights at the Hungry Bear over that cobbler. I think I even started one or two.''

''Our competition would kill for that recipe. They've tried to infiltrate several times.'' Intent, she leaned forward and whispered, ''I'm one of only three people who know the entire recipe.''

He had to swallow the sudden lump in his throat at her closeness. Several strands of pale blond hair curled around her delicate face, and her soft blue eyes shone with mystery. He leaned in, nearly brushed his lips against her. ''God, women in power really turn me on.''

''Jerk.'' She pushed on his chest and shoved him back. When she started to stand, he laughed and took hold of her arms.

''Lighten up, Faith. I'm teasing. Now finish telling me what happened in Boston with Digger.''

With a sigh, she settled back, her demeanor subdued. "He left one day, supposedly on a trip to Texas. But he never came back. He gave all his recipes to Parnell Grayson, his manager, and told him to run the shop. Parnell was a brilliant businessman. Before long there were several sandwich shops, all successful. Then one year later, the first Elijah Jane Restaurant. Digger held onto ownership, managed the financial end from Texas, worked out new recipes and items for the menus, but he also gave Parnell exclusive control. The rest, as they say, is history."

It was possible. He'd only been a kid at the time, but Sam remembered some talk about Digger living in Boston for a few months. "What happens now, with Digger gone?"

Faith shook her head. "No one really knows. Parnell is retiring as president, the board is in an upheaval and all new projects are being shelved for the time being. Until Digger's death is official and his will is read, everything is on hold."

"So the wolves are all waiting to see how Digger's millions get split up," he said tightly. "How much do you expect to get, Miss Courtland?"

"There's a lot more at stake here than money, Mr. McCants." Fire sparked in her cool blue eyes. "I've worked at Elijah Jane since I was sixteen. Weekends, nights, summer vacations. After I graduated, sixty-hour weeks were short hours for me. I'm the one who started the frozen food line, who brought advertising to TV, who personally opened ten restaurants in three states."

Sam raised a brow. "You're an ambitious woman, Faith. Or should I say Madam President?"

Her cheeks turned pink and that cute little chin of

hers lifted. "I've worked for it, I was next in line. But only Digger had the power to appoint a new president. If the board votes, my chances are somewhere between slim and none."

"If you've worked as hard as you say, earned the position, why wouldn't they vote you in?"

The look she gave him was indulgent, and more than a little patronizing. "In case you haven't noticed, and I do believe you have, I'm a woman, and I'm young. Even on a ranch, I'm sure that would be a disadvantage."

Not for what he had in mind, Sam thought, but was smart enough to keep that thought to himself.

She was holding something back, playing some kind of game here. He was certain of it. He accepted that she thought him a country bumpkin, a cowboy who thought the term stock meant cattle and marketing meant buying groceries. He didn't much give a damn what Faith Courtland thought about his business acumen, but he sure as hell didn't like being made to look like a fool.

"None of this really answers why *you're* here," he said evenly. "Wills are legal documents. It would have made more sense if one of Elijah Jane's lawyers had met with me. So tell me what made *you,* a busy woman with a lot of responsibility, decide to come all the way out here?"

She stared at the computer for a long moment, then sighed and leaned back in the chair. "Without a body, Digger can't be declared legally dead until the State approves the petition. The company will be in chaos, the board will battle for control, stock prices will plummet. I intend to make sure that doesn't happen."

Evening had veiled the room in near darkness now. The light from the computer screen cast a golden glow on Faith's soft features. Sam could see the exhaustion in her eyes, but there was an underlying determination. "And just how do you intend to do that, Miss Courtland?"

Determination overcame exhaustion as she leaned forward and looked up at him. "I intend to find Digger's body."

Three

"You intend to do *what?*"

"He's out there somewhere." She pulled off her glasses, dropped them back in her purse. "I intend to find him."

Based on the serious tone in her voice and that stubborn little tilt of her chin he'd already come to recognize, Sam thought it best not to laugh. "A search team already combed the area. Twice. The force of a flash flood in a canyon is without mercy. It takes everything in its path. Digger's camp was directly in that path, almost entirely washed away. There was no sign of him or his horse. His body could be miles away, under dirt and rocks."

Faith's face went pale. He hadn't meant to be so blunt, but under the absurdity of what she was suggesting, there seemed to be no other way.

"*Could be* miles away," she repeated his words with a catch in her voice. "But you don't know for sure, do you?"

"Of course we don't know for sure. We'll never know anything about what happened for sure. Life's like that sometimes. You just accept it and go on."

She shook her head. "I can't accept it."

"Darlin', you don't have any choice."

"There are always choices," she said firmly. "Some people are simply more active in their decisions."

He narrowed his eyes. "I was down in that canyon for six days straight with two different search-and-rescue teams. Nobody knows the Lonesome Rock area better than me."

"Then *you* take me in."

Startled at her suggestion, all he could do was stare. She *was* serious. She wanted to go into Lonesome Rock Canyon, and she wanted him to take her.

"I've been riding since I was five," she went on. "I know how to handle a horse. Please, Sam, take me into the canyon."

His name on her lips was a quiet plea. When she leaned in close to him, her eyes imploring, he felt his insides twist. It would be absolutely ridiculous, foolish even, to waste his time, or hers. But then—he thought of those long legs and curvy hips—he realized there could certainly be worse ways to spend a few days.

"I'll pay you anything you want."

She might as well have poured ice water down his pants. Money. Everything with Faith Courtland seemed to be about money or business. He mentally kicked himself to think he had nearly lost his sanity to those blue eyes.

"Sorry, Ms. Courtland." He almost felt a touch of regret. Almost. "Not interested. You're just going to have to learn how to deal with your business problems some other way."

Her shoulders went as rigid as her voice. "If you won't take me, I'll just hire someone else."

He shrugged. "It's your money. Waste it any way you choose. I suggest you don't try to hire anyone from these parts, though. You tell anyone that you're going into the mountains to look for Digger's body because his two-hundred-million-dollar business is in trouble and they'll put you in a padded cell."

"You can't stop me from looking for him," she said coolly.

"Who said anything about stopping you?" He felt unreasonably angry. "That's your unofficial fiancé's job. And speaking of him, I'd like to know what kind of a man would let his wife-to-be go traipsing off into the mountains with a strange guy?"

Imperceptibly, her chin rose higher. "Harold is extremely understanding. He would never presume to tell me what to do. Our relationship is based on mutual trust and respect."

"Mutual stupidity, is more like it." He grabbed both arms of the chair she sat in, effectively caging her in. "That would be the day I'd let the woman I loved go off with another man."

She held her calm gaze level with his, but Sam could have sworn the pulse at the base of her neck was trembling. He felt strangely torn between wringing that gorgeous neck and kissing it.

"I'm not 'going off' with anyone." Icicles hung from her words. "And fortunately, your antiquated attitude toward the modern woman has nothing to do with me. I don't like loose ends, Mr. McCants. Especially where Elijah Jane is concerned. Once this matter can be put to rest, the company can proceed smoothly and effectively. Now if you'll excuse me, I have a great deal of paperwork I've brought with me and several phone calls to make."

He knew when he'd been dismissed. Damn if this foolish woman didn't know how to test a man's patience. His hands tightened around the arms of the chair, and he leaned closer to her. The flicker of fear in her eyes gave him tremendous satisfaction. "What will you do, Faith," he murmured, "if you do go off into those mountains with the wrong man?"

"Well, Mr. McCants—" her breathing had deepened, but she didn't budge or look away "—I guess I'll just have to make sure that doesn't happen."

"Jake Stone," Savannah softly chided her husband, "our guest has been here at least two full minutes and she hasn't a drink in her hand. Shame on you."

Faith, still recovering from Jake's bear hug greeting and Savannah's warm welcome, barely had time to open her mouth and decline before Jessica, Jake's younger sister, pressed a glass of white wine into her hand.

"The boy's slow, but harmless," Jessica said, referring to her brother. Then she handed her husband Dylan a bottle of beer. The baby boy in his arms leaned close, mouth open and ready to clamp onto the bottle. "You give our son a taste of that beer, Dylan Grant, and you'll spend the next week sleeping in that shed you're building behind the jail in Makeshift."

Dylan and the baby both looked disappointed, until Jared walked in carrying a blond-curled toddler wearing a darling denim dress. Annie, who looked even more pregnant than the day before, waved off Jake and Jessica's offer of assistance.

There were more greetings, more hugs, more kisses. No kiss-the-air, stiff-backed hellos that Faith was used to, but rib-crunching hugs and loud smacks on the cheeks that made her head spin.

She nearly had the names straight when a beautiful young girl around thirteen years old came into the living room with a pink-cheeked, dark-haired toddler perched on one slender hip. The teenager, with her dark hair and deep blue eyes, looked like Jessica's clone.

"This is our sister Emma." Jake kissed the youngest Stone sibling on the top of her head, then scooped up the toddler, who shrieked with delight as she was tossed up in the air. "And this is Madeline."

Without warning, Jake pushed the laughing child into Faith's free arm.

"Swift work, brother-in-law." Annie fell into the couch with a sigh. "Throw your daughter up in the air, then hand her over to your guest whose gorgeous pantsuit is not only white, but also happens to be a Peter Nygard."

From the blank expression on Jake's face, Annie might as well have been speaking a foreign language. Faith suddenly felt out of place here again, wishing she'd worn something more casual. Which would have been impossible, since she hadn't brought anything casual.

But her wardrobe seemed to be the least of her worries right now. Afraid to move, afraid to breathe, she stared at the baby in her arms. She'd never been around babies before. She'd never even held one. The cherub grinned at her and bounced up and down, wanting to be tossed in the air again. She smelled wonderful, Faith thought. Like baby shampoo and soap. Madeline pushed the end of Faith's nose with one chubby finger.

"You're supposed to honk," Jared offered.

Honk? Self-conscious, she uttered a tiny squeak that sounded more like a pig. Madeline didn't seem to mind, though. She giggled with delight and pushed Faith's nose again. Warming to the toddler, Faith gave it another go, then laughed herself when Madeline squealed in pleasure.

That's how Sam found Faith when he walked in. Standing in the middle of Jake's living room, dressed like a goddess in white, holding a giggling baby in one arm, a glass of wine in the other, honking like a goose.

Damn, but the woman was beautiful.

"Don't look now, Ms. Courtland." Sam grinned and touched the brim of his black Stetson as Faith's head snapped in his direction. "Jared's got the video camera."

Eyes wide, Faith glanced across the room. Her playful expression turned to one of alarm as she realized that Jared, indeed, was recording her ridiculous—but adorable, Sam thought—honking.

That's when Madeline decided to throw up.

Everyone—everyone except Faith—moved quickly. Body rigid, she stood frozen while Jake gently removed his daughter—who seemed no worse for wear, just a little confused over what all the fuss was about—and Emma ran to get towels. Savannah, frowning at her husband, led Faith, who appeared to be in shock, into the other room, with Jessica clucking her tongue behind. Annie gave Jake an I-told-you-so look, and he hightailed it out of the room with his daughter. Laughing, Dylan followed, his own son in his arms.

Jared kept filming.

"You get that on tape?" Sam asked Jared, who nodded over his camera but, in light of his wife's glare, knew better than to smile. "I'll pay you a roundup's take on my cattle for a copy of that."

"You should both be horsewhipped," Annie said irritably, shifting her heavy weight on the couch. "I'd do it myself, if I could move."

"She gets a little more cranky every day as her due date gets closer," Jared said good-humoredly. "The last two weeks she was pregnant with Tonya I'd have to wave a white flag before I came in the house at night."

"Stop talking about me as if I'm not here." She fluffed a pillow behind her back. "So I'm a little moody. It comes with the territory."

Foreign territory, Sam thought. All this marriage and baby stuff was alien to him. He was a man much more interested in taking trips where he knew how to speak the language.

Faith Courtland, on the other hand, he thought, watching her as she came back into the room several minutes later, was a woman that could make a man forget how to speak at all.

Savannah had loaned Faith a faded denim shirt that accentuated the blue of her eyes. The jeans she wore were loose on her long legs, but snug on her hips and behind. Even the old black cowboy boots she had on looked as if she'd been born to wear them. She'd gone from goddess-in-white to cowgirl-in-blue in a matter of minutes. Sam couldn't decide which he thought was sexier.

"There's Texas in this girl's blood," Jessica said with a toss of her long dark hair. "All she needs now is a hat."

Sam stepped up to her and slipped his Stetson on her head. It was way too big, of course, but the oversized black hat, set against her light blond hair stirred his blood. He took a step back, not sure if it was for her protection or his.

Cheeks flushed, she smiled as she ran her hands over the brim of the hat. He'd seen that kind of pleasure in a woman's eyes over a dozen red roses, but never a hat. He felt a swift stab of possessiveness, as if her wearing his Stetson was a form of ownership on his part. After a long moment, she lifted the hat off her head and handed it back to him. Their eyes held briefly and her blush deepened.

"I'm sorry to be such a bother," she said to Savannah, who was looking strangely at Sam. "You've all been so kind."

"It was my daughter who messed your beautiful jacket and my husband who caused it." She threw a scolding glance at Jake, who'd come back sheepishly into the room, his daughter clean and fresh in a new pink jumper. "We'll have your jacket cleaned and sent to your hotel. And you can keep the jeans and shirt. I could squeeze into them if I really wanted to, but since my babies I'm not into torture."

"Oh, I couldn't," Faith said quickly, but Sam could see that she wanted to, very badly.

"I insist." Savannah started for the kitchen, calling behind her, "Food's on the table in five everyone. Round up the troops."

Sunday dinner with the Stone family was an event to behold. Fried chicken piled high on a huge platter, bowls heaped with mashed potatoes, rich, thick gravy, biscuits so fluffy that Faith didn't care if she broke every sense of propriety and asked for a second.

Food had always been her business. She'd eaten at restaurants in more than twenty states and four countries, tested recipes from the finest chefs in the world, but she couldn't ever remember a better meal than the one she was having then. She was definitely going to have to finagle some recipes out of Savannah.

It was a bit overwhelming: the bowls coming round, plates getting passed, arms reaching over arms to grab for another piece of chicken or scoop of mashed potatoes. Dinner at her parents' house had always been formal. The attire, the dishes and silverware, the proper wine. Conversation was polite, no one ever shouted or talked when someone else was speaking. Here, with two babies, two toddlers, one teenager and eight adults, there was so much chatter and laughing that Faith felt giddy.

But there was much more to her giddy feeling than the Stone family, Faith admitted to herself. The man sitting in the chair beside her, flirting outrageously with the women and arguing incessantly with the men, seemed to be the cause of her light-headedness.

She knew she should be angry at him. Not only because he'd refused to take her into the mountains, but because he didn't take her seriously. He'd even called her stupid, which was truly unforgivable.

Still, when he'd put his hat on her earlier she'd been overcome by a strange sense of intimacy, as if he'd given her his high school pin, or his letterman's jacket. She'd even felt a sense of loss when she'd handed it back to him. And since they'd sat down to dinner, every time he'd accidentally brushed up against her or their hands had touched while passing a bowl, she'd felt as if a spark of electricity were passing through her.

She knew it was silly, of course. Even foolish. Which only deepened her annoyance. She was twenty-six years old, an almost engaged woman, not a school girl. And she was here in Cactus Flat for Elijah Jane, not for herself.

"Faith, has Sam told you about the time Jake and him dumped Texas Tom's HellFire Pepper Sauce in Digger's ketchup bottles at the Hungry Bear?" Jared asked, grinning.

Faith swiveled to look at Sam, who was frowning at Jared. Jake frowned, as well. "I don't believe I've heard that story."

"They must have been about fourteen at the time," Jared continued, enjoying himself at Jake and Sam's expense. "They watched through Digger's big glass window all day, expecting all the customers to breathe fire and blow smoke out their ears. But nothing happened. No fire, no smoke. No screams of agony. Later in the day they came back in, confused but hungry from watching all those people eat, and Digger fixed them two big burgers, on the house, dripping with his secret sauce. It took them both a couple of bites before it hit, but when it did—'' Jared said, grinning ''—it was like an explosion.''

''A nuclear explosion.'' Sam reached for his water glass as if he were reliving the horror. ''Seems that Digger had seen us spike his ketchup, so he exchanged the bottles, then set us up. Wars could be ended with whatever it was he put in those burgers.''

Jake nodded in agreement. ''I thought I'd have a permanent hole in the top of my head. Which was only the beginning of our torture. We paid for that one…two days straight in the john.''

''Jake!'' Savannah's tone was strict, but her eyes were laughing. ''That's no talk for the dinner table.''

The stories continued: Digger's famed baseball bat pursuit of the deputy sheriff; his abduction of Moses Swain's pig who'd repeatedly destroyed Digger's tomato plants behind the café and Digger's subsequent special on pork chops; his constant meddling in everyone's business that he called ''free advice.'' Everyone laughed so hard Dylan spit water and Jessica got the hiccups.

''Enough,'' Annie said, wiping at the tears in her eyes with one hand while she held her side with the other. ''I swear, I'll have this baby right here and damn if that wouldn't be Digger's fault.''

''There wasn't a wedding that took place—'' Jessica said, wiping mashed potatoes off her son's chin ''—a baby born, or business deal in Cactus Flat that Digger didn't somehow take credit for. Even you,

Faith. He's probably looking down at us, taking credit for you being here right now."

The sudden change in Faith's demeanor was subtle, almost imperceptible, but Sam caught it nonetheless. The slight angling of her chin, her stiff smile. Why in the world would Jessica's harmless comment bother the woman?

"Now, *Sam* here," Jake said, pushing his plate away as he eyed a pecan pie sitting on the sideboard, "he was Digger's greatest challenge. Sam's marital status to Digger was like a red flag to a bull."

"Not to mention every woman within a five-hundred mile radius," Savannah added, making room on the table for pie and cookies.

"Once all you ladies were taken, I resigned myself to a life of celibacy." Sam's look was forlorn, his wink at Savannah wicked. There were groans around the table, with Jake nearly choking.

"Why, even Faith here is taken," Sam said. "Practically engaged to Howard from Boston. Isn't that right, Faith?"

She threw him a sharp glance. "Harold."

"Right." Pleased with himself and the mischief he was causing, Sam accepted the slice of pecan pie that Savannah handed him. "He's extremely understanding, she tells me."

Her glance turned to a glare. "As a matter of fact, he is."

"A rare quality in a man," Annie said.

Jared, who'd been nibbling on a cookie his daughter had offered him from her high chair, feigned hurt. "I'm understanding," he complained. "Aren't I, guys?"

The men all nodded and mumbled praise amongst themselves. Jessica rolled her eyes and smiled at Faith. "I'm not sure if I should offer congratulations or condolences. Have you set a date yet?"

"Later this year."

That was a vague answer, Sam thought, satisfied that he'd turned the table talk away from his marital status and pointed it directly at Faith's. He would have liked to pursue the topic during dessert, but Madeline's overturned glass of milk, and Daniel's spoon banging on his high chair made coherent conversation nearly impossible. Dishes were cleared at warp speed, babies were carted off by daddies to prepare for bed, and all the ladies, including Faith and a waddling Annie, disappeared into the kitchen.

Sam stood in the dining room, alone, trying to decide. Join the daddies and babies, or the ladies?

Ladies.

He'd no more than walked into the kitchen before Savannah, who'd been politely refusing Faith's offer of help, took his arm and smoothly guided the two of them out the backdoor and onto a porch swing. Smiling, she waved behind her, and vanished back into the kitchen.

The moon was nearly full, bright enough to illuminate Jake's corral and barn and cast long shadows off the trees in the backyard. And stars. Faith couldn't remember when she'd ever seen so many. She rarely got out of the city when she was home, and when she'd traveled, she'd never had the time to simply sit and look up at the sky. The night was warm, the air filled with the sound of crickets and the scent of gardenias blooming in pots on the patio.

Sam, with one arm stretched casually behind her and the other thrown over the back of the swing, began a slow, rhythmic rocking.

The tension she'd felt sitting next to him all evening—and the annoyance—melted away with each unhurried sway of the swing. With a sigh, she leaned back and looked up at the night sky. "They're wonderful."

"The stars?"

"The Stones, all of them."

"Even little Maddy?" He grinned at her.

Faith smiled. "Of course. She's just a baby, for heaven's sake. Do you think I'd care more about a little mess on my clothes than a precious darling like that?"

He studied her for a moment, then lifted his gaze to the sky. "As far back as I can remember, they've been more like family to me than just neighbors."

"What about your family? You have brothers or sisters?"

He shook his head. "My mom died when I was ten, my dad five years ago. Jake and Jared and Jessica, we all grew up together. They've always been there for me. Except that little strip of time that Jake mistakenly thought I'd made improper advances toward his first wife. We straightened all that up a few years back."

There was no question Sam was a ladies' man, Faith thought, but somehow she didn't see him messing with another man's wife. "I can't imagine Jake and Savannah ever being with anyone else. They're wonderful together. So are Jared and Annie, and Jessica and Dylan. I've never seen couples more in love."

He raised his eyebrows and glanced at her. "What about you and Arnold? Aren't you in love?"

"*Harold.*" She was too relaxed to let him goad her. "And of course we're in love. He's the perfect man."

"Perfect, huh? What's so perfect about him?"

"Well, for one thing, he'd never butt into anyone's business and ask personal questions." Some people might think Harold indifferent, maybe a little dry at times, but she understood he had a lot on his mind. "He's an accountant with a large legal firm, a gentleman of the highest caliber, patient and even-tempered."

"You call that perfect?" Sam started to laugh. "A perfect bore, maybe."

Bristling, Faith shifted deeper into the swing and folded her arms. "He also takes me seriously, another important quality."

Sam let his arm slip down lower and the tips of his fingers brushed the back of her neck. "I take you seriously."

"Sure you do."

"I do, darlin'. Real serious."

His eyes sobered as he looked at her. There was no amusement now, no laughter. What she did see made her breath catch. Desire. Lust. She was torn between amazement and terror, and she couldn't help but wonder if he affected all women this way.

But then, she already knew the answer to that. Of course he did.

The sudden race of her heart didn't mean a thing,

Faith told herself. Or that fluttering in her stomach. A mild attraction, maybe. She was relaxed, there were thousands of stars overhead. She was bound to have some kind of reaction to this man's blatant virility. She could handle it. In spite of the shiver making its way up her spine as Sam's fingers lightly moved over her shoulders, she was perfectly capable of keeping a clear head.

"Sam, if you mean that, then I want you to take me."

He went still, even his fingers on her neck were motionless. "Take you?"

That hadn't come out quite right. "Into the mountains," she added quickly. "To Lonesome Rock Canyon."

He swore softly, then continued his lazy swinging of the bench. "You don't give up, do you?"

"Do you?" She leaned toward him. "If there was something you desperately needed to do, and you were the only one who could make it happen, would you just give up, even if the odds were against you and you might make a fool out of yourself?"

He stopped the rocking again and stared down at her. "Yeah," he drawled, his gaze dropping to her lips, "I see what you mean."

He moved so quickly she had no time to catch her breath, let alone think. His mouth covered hers, his kiss as possessive as it was urgent. He pressed her back against the swing, his tongue tasting, searching, then mating with hers. She made a small, helpless sound, trembled, then shocked herself by surrendering.

Sensation after sensation swept through her. Hot.

Cold. Dizzy. And that strange little knot of need tightening low in her belly, that was certainly new to her. Unable to keep still, her fingers stroked his thick, dark hair. Incredible, she thought dimly as she moved her hands over his head, even the texture of his hair had a sensuous feel to it.

He deepened the kiss, pulling her against him. She felt herself melt against him, even moaned softly as his hands skimmed up her sides.

The sound of laughing from inside the kitchen startled her from the insanity possessing her. Though her body told her to proceed full speed ahead, her mind was back at the helm. She pushed him away.

"Sam," she said breathlessly, "that's exactly my point. You aren't taking any of this seriously."

"You're wrong there, darlin'." His expression was dark, his jaw tight. "I took that very seriously."

"You know what I mean."

He sighed deeply and shook his head. "You are one hell of a woman, Faith Courtland, and of all the places I want to take you, not one of them involve hiking or camping or searching for bodies that are best left alone. My answer is still no."

He had to be the most frustrating, impossible man she'd ever met. She stood, needing to leave quickly before she either told him to go to hell, or begged him to kiss her again.

"Until tomorrow morning, then," she said calmly, praying her knees wouldn't give out on her. "Nine o'clock?"

"Nine is fine. Just like you." He winked at her.

She pressed her lips tightly together, afraid she might smile at his silly compliment and encourage him. She had all she could handle with him as he was.

She'd be herself tomorrow. Fully rested, focused and in control. And as soon as they went over Digger's will and got the particulars in order, she would finally be free of Mr. Sam McCants.

Sam pulled his truck into the parking lot of the Cactus Flat First National Bank and switched off the engine. Clouds darkened the west horizon and threatened rain, but for the moment, the sky overhead was a deep blue, and a light breeze rippled the flag in front of the bank.

Nine o'clock sharp.

He'd been up since five. The cattle in the south pasture had needed to be moved, and he'd helped his foreman, Clayton, and three other hands round up the herd and move them to the east pasture. With the workload so light this time of year, they hadn't really needed his help, but what the hell. He'd been wide-awake most of the night anyway, thanks to a curvy blonde with baby-blue eyes.

He'd known those soft, sweet lips would be sweet, but he'd never expected the punch in the gut that came with them. One kiss and she'd released something in him that bordered on violent. He'd struggled to contain the need she'd aroused in him, to leash the impulse to drag her down on that swing and really kiss her like he'd wanted to. To unbutton her blouse and slide his hands over her smooth, silky skin.

At that moment, all he'd wanted was her in his bed...and all she'd wanted was him to take her on an excursion in the mountains to look for dead bodies.

He'd felt her tremble, though, dammit. For a minute, when she'd forgotten herself, let herself go, she'd been like warm taffy in his hands. His male pride was slightly compensated by that knowledge, but only slightly. If he wanted to keep his self-respect intact, he'd better listen to that little voice that told him to keep his distance from one Faith Courtland.

She rose from the chair she'd been waiting in when he stepped inside the bank. Her navy-blue suit was conservative, skirt to the knees and pumps low, the white blouse underneath her loose jacket simple. She wore her wire-rimmed glasses and had pulled her hair back into a snug little bun. Her only concession to femininity was a single strand of pearls around her neck.

Bank image, Sam decided. And while he liked her much better in tight jeans and little black skirts with high heels, there was also something appealing about this severe style. Something that stimulated his imagination overtime and made him wonder how she would look wearing nothing but those pearls and glasses, her hair tumbling over her shoulders as he slowly pulled the pins from that cute little bun.

Cheered by the image, he smiled brightly and tipped his hat to her. "Mornin'."

Her smile was stiff. "Good morning."

Jennifer Summers, manager of business accounts, emerged from behind the counter and sauntered over to him. "Hi, Sam. Haven't seen you for a while."

Sam had taken the pretty brunette to dinner…what? Two, three weeks ago? No, more like a month. He'd meant to give her a call. "Been a little busy at the ranch. Should be lightening up soon, though.'' He smiled.

She smiled back, twisting a long strand of hair, then straightened as she realized that Faith was staring coldly at her. ''Oh. Miss Courtland. You were waiting for Sam—I mean, Mr. McCants—weren't you?''

''I need to get into my safe deposit box, Jen.'' Sam handed her his key. ''And if it's possible, can Miss Courtland and I use your private office?''

''Of course.'' Her smile was back. ''Can I get you something, coffee...tea?''

Faith almost expected the woman to say, *or me.* No doubt, that was what the attractive bank manager who'd barely said hello to her when she'd walked into the bank several minutes ago had *wanted* to say to Sam. For heaven's sake, did every woman who met Sam McCants fall for his rugged good looks and cowboy charm?

What a stupid thing to wonder. Of course every woman did. *She* had, hadn't she?

She remembered the feel of his lips against hers last night, the slide of his hand over her waist, the pressure of his hard body against hers—

''Faith?''

Sam and Jennifer both stood looking at her. Sam had already come out of the vault and held his metal safety deposit box in his hand.

She cleared her throat, hoping the heat she felt on her neck hadn't yet reached her cheeks, and followed them into an office at the back of the bank.

''Just call if you need me,'' Jennifer said, but Faith had the distinct feeling that the pretty bank officer wasn't just referring to right now.

Sam pulled up a chair for Faith, then sat across the desk from her. A little knot began to build in her stomach as he opened the box and pulled out a legal-sized brown envelope sealed with clear tape. When he broke the seal, then pulled out two sheets of lined paper, the knot in her stomach tightened.

Sam looked up at her, then back at the paper in his hand and began to read aloud:

"Dear Sam,

Well, son, if you're reading this then I have to assume that the time had finally come for this old geezer to move on. I know everyone thought I was too damn ornery to ever go, but I never did fancy being predictable to folks, neither. Man's gotta have a few surprises, don't you think?

By now, I'm sure you've discovered at least one of them surprises—Elijah Jane Corporation. You're thinking someone's pulling your leg, right? No, siree, son, it's the God's truth. Imagine an old codger like me tied up with a company like Elijah Jane. Ain't it a hoot? Even I never quite believed it myself all these years.

Sam, you and the Stones were about as close to family as I ever got. I know you got a level head on them shoulders and I trust you to see that my assets are cared for. But there is one thing I'm going to ask of you, Sam, one thing real important to me. In exchange, Matilda will get the diner, with her salary tripled for the next twenty years and a pension, and you, son, well, I'm gonna give you something you've always wanted—that twenty-thousand acres you been trying to buy east of the Circle B. Another surprise. I bought that parcel twenty-seven years ago, thinking I might finally settle down. Luck wasn't with me, but I kept the land anyway, under another name, hoping someday it might come in handy.

Well, Sam that someday is here now and this is what I'd like you to do for me."

Sam stopped and looked at Faith. The knot in her stomach felt more like a lump now. Her fingers clutched the arms of her chair. "Go on," she whispered.

Eyes still locked on her, he read,

"I want you to marry the vice-president of Elijah Jane, Miss Faith Courtland, who also happens to be my daughter."

Four

The faint ringing of a telephone from somewhere in the bank was the only sound in the small office. Faith sat unmoving, unblinking, her face rigid. "*What* did you say?"

Her words were a throaty whisper, barely audible even in the quiet. But then, Sam was having a tough time finding words himself. "You're Digger Jones's *daughter?*"

"That part I heard, and already knew." Color splashed her pale cheeks. "It's the you-marry-me part I'm a little confused about."

"Well, I'm a hell of a lot more than a *little* confused, darlin'. Digger Jones is your father, and he wants me to *marry* you?"

She pressed her lips tightly together. "I assure you, I'm just as surprised as you are. Why don't you finish reading, then we'll discuss this?"

Discuss this? A bombshell had just been dropped in their laps and she just sat there, steady as a rock. Did anything ever rattle this woman, for God's sake?

At the sound of a short knock on the door, Faith jumped and for a moment, only a moment, Sam saw the panic in her eyes. Not so calm and cool after all, he thought, and when Jennifer stuck her head in the door, he reassured the brunette that he and Miss Courtland were doing just fine.

Like hell they were.

When Jennifer closed the door again, Sam picked up the will and continued.

> ''Faith is a good woman, Sam. Dependable, responsible. Steady and strong, not to mention a real looker. I've watched her grow up with Elijah Jane, not in person, but still, I've become very fond of her, as I am of you. Nothing would make me happier than to see you two young'uns hitched. However, I know you are both stubborn as mules, so I've taken a few matters into my own hands, for your own good, of course. Just two months, that's all I'm asking. A legal marriage for two months, under the same roof. You get the land and Faith gets what I know she wants—the presidency of Elijah Jane, along with all my voting shares and corporate assets. If the marriage don't work out in that time, you each go your own way. The land still belongs to you, Elijah Jane to Faith, and the diner and salary to Matilda.
>
> ''Well, son, I don't envy you none, having to explain this to Faith. Needless to say, she won't

like it much and has an independent streak in her that reminds me too much of yours truly. But who knows, Sammy boy, in two months, the both of you just might thank me.''

Thank him? Struck dumb, Sam laid the will down and leaned back in his chair. Faith stared at him, her expression emotionless, then stood and moved to the window overlooking the parking lot. ''We'll contest it, of course,'' she said. ''Obviously he wasn't in his right mind.''

He watched her fold her arms, a protective gesture, as if she were holding herself together physically as well as emotionally. ''How long have you known that Digger was your father?''

''Biological father only.'' She pressed a hand to her temple and sighed. ''My mother told me three weeks ago, shortly after we learned that Digger had died. They'd kept in touch over the years, she'd even orchestrated my getting a job at Elijah Jane when I was a teenager. She knew that Digger had made you executor of his estate. He'd left your name with her as a contact, even told her he'd left a will with you.''

''So why the hell didn't you tell me that he was your father?''

''I had no reason to, at least not until I heard what was in Digger's will. Besides, would you have believed me?''

Would he have believed her? He barely accepted the fact that Digger owned Elijah Jane Corporation. Not in a million years would he have thought Digger Jones had a daughter.

He swore softly, let out a deep breath. "You want to tell me about it?"

For a few moments she continued to stare silently out the window, and when she finally spoke, her voice was even, controlled.

"My grandfather, Hayden Buchanan, owned an investment company in downtown Boston, a prestigious firm with influential and extremely wealthy clients. My mother, Colleen, worked there, just part-time, busy work to fill the hours between the socialite luncheons and charity functions that were expected of her. One of her more important duties was to pick up sandwiches at lunchtime."

The sarcasm in Faith's voice was not difficult to detect. She turned from the window, a distant look in her eyes. "My mother told me that for her it was love at first sight. It didn't matter that he was older. She thought Digger looked like Sean Connery and Kirk Douglas both rolled into one."

Sam raised his eyebrows. "Now I *know* you've got the wrong guy."

Faith smiled. "Even my mother said the edges were rough, but that was what made him all the more attractive to her. She never missed a day picking up sandwiches. After a while, they started to see each other. Secretly, of course. My grandparents would never have allowed their only daughter to date a man who made sandwiches for a living. They had the son of a wealthy client picked out for her, and were anxious for her to marry. She was already twenty-seven. Old by their standards."

"Ancient." In spite of the seriousness of the situation, Sam couldn't help himself.

She ignored his dig, then continued, "They planned to marry, even without my grandparents' approval. But Digger wanted to make a home for them first, in Texas. She agreed to wait for him while he went back to make the arrangements. My grandparents found out about their plans and put a stop to them, then forced my mother to marry the man they'd already chosen, Joseph Courtland III. Joseph was ambitious, so it made no difference to him that my mother was carrying another man's baby. He got a promotion, along with the honored position as son-in-law in one of Boston's wealthiest families."

Sam shook his head. "I know Digger, he would never—"

"No, Sam, you don't know Digger." Her voice was sharp now. "And neither do I. And it doesn't matter, anyway. Whatever happened twenty-seven years ago, happened. Right now, we need to deal with the issue at hand."

Not for a second did Sam believe that Faith thought it didn't matter. It mattered big time. But for now, he'd let it go. "You mean the 'issue' of me marrying you."

"It's absolutely idiotic."

It *was* absurd, of course, but Sam's ego winced at her verbal jab nonetheless. He restrained the urge to tell her that there were a few ladies who might disagree with her opinion. "Of course it is."

She stared at the paper lying on the desk, then looked at Sam. "You have a lawyer in town?"

"Ethan Mitchell."

She walked back to the desk. This time, Sam noticed her legs shook slightly. She picked up the phone and handed it to him. "Tell him we're on our way."

Faith definitely was not having a good day.

She sat in a booth at the Hungry Bear Café, heard the voices of the lunch crowd around her and the clink of silverware, smelled the hamburgers grilling and the coffee brewing, but she felt numb to all of it. As if her body were sitting here, but her mind were floating in a fog.

She struggled to pull herself out of that fog, to piece together everything that had happened that morning and understand what the lawyer had explained to her and Sam. A handwritten, or holographic will, Ethan Mitchell had said, was perfectly legal. As long as every word on the document was written in the deceased's own hand, on a blank sheet of paper, with the conditions spelled out clearly, it was valid. Unfortunately, Digger had met all the criteria for the will to be legal and binding.

And that wasn't the worst of it.

The first problem was that there was no body. The state would have to approve the petition, which they most probably would, Ethan felt, but that could take several months. And as far as the marriage arrangement went, Ethan's advice was to comply with the terms. By the time the petition for death was approved, the two months would already be passed, and they could go ahead and get an annulment or divorce—then inherit. To contest the will would only delay matters further, cost more money and no doubt bring the case under public scrutiny.

And that was something Faith definitely didn't want.

With a heavy sigh, she leaned back in the booth and watched Sam talking on the pay phone at the back of the restaurant. He'd leaned one shoulder against the wall, his head down as he spoke quietly, his black Stetson hiding his expression from her.

He'd handled all this very well, she thought. Certainly much better than she had. She'd been teetering on the edge of hysteria all day, though she'd be damned if she'd let Sam McCants know that. The future president of Elijah Jane didn't cry, or scream or throw things. Everything that she'd wanted to do as she sat in that office and listened to Sam read Digger's will.

Anger broke through the fog enveloping her. How dare Digger do this to her! Wasn't it enough that he'd left her mother, pregnant and alone—abandoned the woman he supposedly loved and his own child? Why now, after almost twenty-seven years, was he interfering in the life of a daughter he'd never known? That he'd chosen not to know? And what right did he have to pick a man for her or to set down ultimatums?

And if he was going to choose a man, why would he choose a man who wouldn't want her, a man who'd made it clear he had no intention of marrying? She and Sam were as different as night and day. How could Digger possibly have believed that she and a bachelor cowboy could possibly be right for each other?

She looked at Sam now, watched as he tipped his hat back and exposed the rugged angles of his face to her. She would at least admit the physical part was there. She was moderately attracted to him, sexually. Oh, all right, she was *extremely* attracted to him. And he did have a certain charm, a way of looking at a woman and smiling that made her insides go soft. She wasn't about to let him know that. His ego was certainly big enough. Every single woman, young or old, who came within fifty yards of the man made googoo eyes. She'd just be one more weak-kneed female if she gave in to his appeal.

"Ain't hard to look at, is he?"

Startled, Faith looked up at the waitress and recognized the platinum blonde from Digger's memorial service. It was Matilda. Heat flooded Faith's face and she glanced quickly away, carefully studying a huge stuffed bear rising ominously over the jukebox in the corner. "I was just looking at the bear," she mumbled.

Matilda laughed, a loud, raucous laugh for such a fragile-looking woman, then set two glasses of water on the table. "No need to be embarrassed, honey. If I was twenty, shoot, make it ten years younger and single, I'd jump that boy's bones and hang on for the ride." The woman leaned in close. "I hear it's a real wild one, too."

Faith coughed, then quickly took a drink of the water. "I really wouldn't know."

"No?" Matilda wrinkled her brow. "The way that boy was looking at you when you come in here, I thought for sure you two were…well, be patient, honey. This might be your lucky day."

Lucky day? Faith nearly choked. *Lucky day?* A tiny scream bubbled in her throat and she was certain that if Sam hadn't suddenly appeared and scooped the waitress up in his arms, that scream would have ripped loose.

When he set the woman down again, she slapped him playfully on the arm, then told him to take his hat off and behave himself. Grinning, he tossed his Stetson on the seat and slid in beside it.

"How's Dodge doing?" Sam asked Matilda, and the concern in his voice didn't slip past Faith.

"That old cuss will outlive us all, less'n I shoot him myself. Sitting in a wheelchair has made him right crabby—that and his male pride 'cause he can't work. But don't you worry none, Sammy, he'll be walking again soon."

Someone in the back of the crowded café hollered for coffee and Matilda hollered right back that it was rude to holler, then turned back to Sam. "What can I get you and your lady?"

"My lady," Sam said, stretching the word out, "will have a burger, loaded, French fries and a chocolate shake. I'll have the same."

"I'm capable of ordering for myself." Faith handed the menu to Matilda. "I'd like a hamburger, an order of French fries and a chocolate shake."

Laughing, Matilda took the menu and winked at Faith. "I'll hold the onions."

"Is Dodge her husband?" Faith asked when the waitress hurried off.

Sam nodded. "He had a tractor roll over him three weeks ago. He's healing up well, but the doctors he's seen aren't sure he'll walk again."

Faith watched the petite dynamo bellow an order to the cook, then joke with a cowboy sitting at the counter as she filled coffee cups. "She's holding it together well."

"Matilda's not one to dwell on what could have been. She's always accepted whatever came her way and made the best of it. If the Hungry Bear closes down, though, she won't have a job."

Frustration made Faith clench her teeth. "Are you going to tell her about the will?"

Sam frowned. "I have to. But not just yet. Not until we have a few things straightened out. Besides," he said, his smile slowly fading, "she doesn't get a dime unless we meet the conditions of Digger's will, remember?"

Faith closed her eyes. "There must be some way to help her and her husband, something we can do, without…without…." She couldn't even say it.

"Getting married?" he supplied, then shook his head. "I've already tried to help, even offered to send Dodge to a specialist in Dallas, but he thinks it's charity and refuses to go."

Faith reached for her water, stared at the ice as she turned the cold glass in her hands. There were too many people caught up in this mess, too many people whose lives would be profoundly affected by whatever decisions were made.

"This land that Digger owns," she said carefully, "the twenty-thousand acres. It's important to you?"

"It's critical for grazing. I've been leasing property from Jake, but his herd has doubled in the past three years and he needs the land back when the extension on my lease runs out next month. I'll have to sell off a good portion of my herd if I don't find more grazing land."

In spite of the noise around them—dishes rattling, people talking, the country and western tune blaring from a jukebox in the corner—Faith felt a sudden calm come over her. She was a business woman, wasn't she? She'd worked out more difficult deals than this one, though certainly none as unusual. If she set aside her emotions, looked at the situation purely from an objective standpoint, then the answer was simple.

Business. That's all this was.

Drawing in a deep breath, she straightened and looked directly at Sam. "So you need the land," she said, folding her hands in her lap. "And I need control at Elijah Jane."

He sat back in the booth, narrowing his eyes. "Are you thinking what I think you're thinking?"

"I can't let everything I've worked for all these years fall apart," she said firmly. "And it isn't as if it would be a real marriage."

"Of course not."

"We wouldn't have to…well…." She blushed.

He lifted one eyebrow. "No, we wouldn't have to."

Her throat felt dry, her heart drummed wildly against her ribs. "Two months. We could manage that."

"Under the same roof," he reminded her. "And I sure as hell am not going to Boston."

"I can work from Digger's computer, with a fax and a phone line."

They studied each other for a long moment, the tension closing around them like a net. He leaned across the table, close enough that she caught the scent of his aftershave, and the even more intoxicating scent that was his alone.

"Miss Courtland—" he said as he took her hands in his and the rough feel of his palms covering her fingers sent sparks skittering up her arms "—are you asking me to marry you?"

She had to swallow before she could continue. "Yes, Mr. McCants. I guess I am."

He moved even closer, and despite the crowded room, despite herself, she leaned toward him. His mouth hovered just above hers, his gaze dropped to her lips. "There *is* something you've forgotten, just a minor complication, I'm sure."

"What's that?" she whispered.

He stared directly into her eyes now, and she saw what she thought was smug satisfaction in his dark gaze. "Arnold."

"Arnold?"

He smiled. "Yeah. That other guy you were supposed to marry."

Harold! With a small gasp, Faith jerked backward, pulling her hands from his. Good heavens, she *had* forgotten about Harold. Damn, damn, damn!

"I—I'll…call him. Once I explain, he'll be fine."

"He'll be fine that you're going to marry another man?" Sam shook his head and rolled his eyes. "Oh, yeah, that's right, I forgot, he's *understanding.*"

"And what about you?" she asked, refusing to let him rattle her any more than she already was. "What will you tell everyone when they ask?"

Sam glanced at Matilda thoughtfully. "It's probably best we don't tell anyone the truth, at least not until later. Matilda will just start hollering about charity again.'' He leaned back in the booth and grinned. ''I'll just tell everyone that you proposed, and I couldn't bear to break your heart.''

She frowned at him. ''If you were a gentleman, you'd say you proposed, and I couldn't bear to break your heart.''

''Darlin', I never said I was a gentleman.'' The wicked gleam in his eyes turned to amusement. ''Okay, how 'bout we fell madly in love and couldn't wait to make it legal?''

''That's half true,'' she conceded. ''The sooner we make this legal, the sooner we'll both have everything we want.''

''Will we?'' The look he gave her was intensely sexual. In spite of herself, in spite of the situation, she felt her insides grow warm and her heart beat faster.

Faith didn't have the voice to reply and was thankful when Matilda reappeared and slid two plates of steaming hamburgers on the table, heaped with golden French fries. Two months wasn't so bad, she told herself, and drew in a deep, calming breath. Eight little weeks. It would be a snap.

Feeling lighter now that the decision was made, she bit into her burger and was amazed that she was actually hungry. The time would pass quickly, she told herself. She'd keep herself so immersed in work that she'd probably hardly ever see Sam. She'd be back in Boston in no time at all, president of Elijah Jane—and Sam McCants would be nothing but a distant memory.

They were married three days later in Horse Bend, a small town thirty miles away. Sam hadn't wanted word to get out before the wedding, so he'd applied for the marriage license in Horse Bend, as well. Jake Stone stood up for him, Savannah for Faith, and the rest of the Stone family were in attendance.

It hadn't been easy for Sam to lie to his friends, but right now the truth about Digger's wealth and his ridiculous will was more unbelievable than the story that he and Faith had fallen in love and couldn't wait to be married. No one needed to know the real reason, not even Jake. Though Sam suspected that his best friend hadn't quite swallowed the "falling madly in love and couldn't wait" story. Sam knew he'd tell Jake the truth eventually, after Faith went back to Boston, he had his twenty-thousand acres, and Matilda the café. They'd all have a good laugh, maybe even smoke a cigar and have a few beers to celebrate his new grazing land. He'd be a contented bachelor again, and Faith could marry Arnold...or Harvey...or whatever the hell the idiot's name was.

And he *was* an idiot, too, Sam thought, watching Faith as Savannah hugged her following the brief ceremony. What man in his right mind would let this woman out of his sight, let alone allow her to marry another man and live in his house, alone, for two months?

His throat had gone dry when she'd walked into the judge's chambers a few minutes ago, her hair swept up on her head, with a few loose curls framing her face. She'd even worn the traditional white, a pretty lace dress that flared around her calves. He assumed her color choice was to convince everyone that she truly was happy to be a bride. The small bouquet of pale pink roses Jessica had brought her matched her cheeks and lips, lips that he'd kissed only moments ago to seal their vows. Soft, lush lips that had trembled slightly under his, forcing him to taste her just a little longer, a little deeper, before he pulled reluctantly away.

She turned to him then, smiling, and if he hadn't known better, he would have thought she actually looked happy—radiant even. Like a woman in love. But it was all a play, he reminded himself, with carefully rehearsed lines and stage directions. They each had something to gain from this marriage, and it had nothing to do with love.

"Come stand by Faith." Annie waved a camera. "I want to take your picture with your wife."

Wife. The word hit him like a fist in his chest. He put his arm around Faith, endured shot after shot, smile after smile, before the group herded them to the town's steak house for a wedding dinner and cake. Whether the Stones believed this was a real marriage or not, they intended to treat it as one.

Too bad Faith didn't feel the same way about the wedding night, Sam thought in frustration. He thought of his big bed at home, and the fact that he'd be sleeping in it alone tonight only increased his frustration. He had images of slipping that pretty lace dress off his bride's soft shoulders and laying her down on that bed, pulling her under him and burying himself deeply into her slender, curvy body until she lost control, until she trembled under him and wanted him as badly as he wanted her.

Cursing silently, he raised his glass for a refill of beer. If he couldn't have Faith in his bed tonight, then he'd settle for a good drunk. She could drive home, he thought irritably. The way she was sipping her champagne, she wouldn't get a buzz till next Tuesday. The cad in him wouldn't mind if she had a little too much to drink and fell into his arms, but in spite of the fact that he wanted her, his pride—and his honor—wanted her sober and willing.

Annie and Jared left the celebration first, with Jared claiming his wife was tired. But the look Annie flashed Savannah and Jessica had Sam wondering if something wasn't afloat. Knowing this group, Sam was keeping his eyes open and watching his back.

Thirty minutes, two slices of cake and three beers later, Sam handed Faith the car keys, stretched out in the front seat of his truck and pulled his Stetson low on his head.

Amazed and delighted that he would let her drive his truck, Faith quickly slid behind the wheel. She felt a little giddy, not from the champagne, just from the celebration in general. The wedding had been like something out of a fantasy. The small town judge, the dress that Savannah had helped her pick out on their shopping trip to Midland, the simple but elegant rose bouquet. It was all so beautiful, so romantic.

And Sam. Her heart fluttered just remembering the smoldering look he'd given her as they'd said their vows. She'd thought him handsome before, but today, dressed in a western-cut black suit, with black shiny boots and Stetson, she'd found him devastating. And when he'd kissed her so tenderly, so sensually, she wondered for one long, breathless moment if she might be making a pact with the devil himself. When he kissed her again, she hadn't cared.

"I've never done this before." She turned the key and the engine roared to life. She was used to a compact and felt small behind the wheel of this massive vehicle.

"Gotten married?" His response was more of a grunt than anything else.

She wondered what he was so surly about, but decided she wasn't going to let him ruin her good mood. "That, too. But I meant drive a truck." She jammed the lever into reverse and the pickup lurched backward.

Sam's hat sailed off and his long legs and arms flew as he righted himself.

"Lord, woman, you trying to kill me?" He reached for his seat belt.

She laughed. "That would make my life much too complicated," she said cheerfully. "Though the Widow McCants does have a certain ring to it, don't you think?"

He settled his hat back on his head and pulled it low, but said nothing, just eased his long muscular body into the seat as she carefully shifted into drive.

"Speaking of rings—" she held up her left hand and the diamond on her third finger sparkled under the lights of the parking lot "—I want to thank you for buying me one. It's really very lovely, but it wasn't necessary."

"What do you mean it wasn't necessary?" he snapped. "What the hell was I supposed to slip on your hand, a pop-up ring from a beer can?"

The cab of the truck seemed to lift straight off the ground and fall back again. Sam scrambled for balance once again, swearing.

"Oops. Speed bump." The back half of the truck suffered the same abuse as she floored the gas pedal and Sam's head hit the roof of the cab. He glared at her. She smiled back. "I'll get the hang of it, don't worry."

Mumbling something incoherent, he jammed his hat on his head again, this time sitting straight, primed and ready.

"I simply meant you needn't have bought me anything so nice. If you can't return it, I'd be happy to reimburse you for it."

"That does it." He turned to stare at her, his face a tight mask of anger. "Stop the truck."

"But—"

"Stop the truck, dammit."

She put it into gear and turned to face him, a little frightened by his sudden outburst, but more confused than anything else. The man was definitely temperamental.

"I can certainly afford to buy *my wife* a ring, dammit. And I sure as hell don't need you to *reimburse* me."

"All right." She nodded. "Thank you, then."

"You're welcome." He folded his arms and looked straight ahead. "And if it eases your mind any, I didn't buy it. It was my mother's."

His mother's? Breath held, she straightened her fingers and stared at the beautiful solitaire surrounded by tiny glittering diamonds. He'd given her his *mother's* ring? That was supposed to ease her mind?

Her throat felt thick; she couldn't speak. She felt the moisture in her eyes, but didn't care. When Harold had given her a ring, she hadn't got mushy or teary-eyed. It had all been so matter-of-fact; just part of the itinerary. She blinked back the tears, struggling to gain control before she did something very foolish. Something like throw herself into Sam's arms and kiss him like any real wife might kiss a real husband.

But she couldn't. Because she wasn't like any other wife, and he wasn't like any other husband. Even the smallest intimate exchange with this man, even a kiss, would be too dangerous. How would they ever make it through two months if their…interaction…became something other than business?

They drove in silence to Sam's ranch, Faith enjoying the power and feel of the truck as it rolled down the highway, Sam staring pensively out the window. Several times she'd felt his heated gaze skim over her, and she'd worked hard to concentrate on the road. The tension filled the cab of the truck like the air before a thunderstorm, growing thicker and stronger. She felt a mixture of relief and renewed apprehension when she finally pulled into the long gravel driveway that led to the Circle B. They'd be out of this truck soon, but then they would be at his house.

Alone.

Palms sweating, she parked in his large circular driveway, then felt her breath catch as she looked at the house.

She didn't know what she'd been expecting, but it certainly wasn't this. This place—his house—was huge, an estate that would rival any manor in the most affluent section of Boston. It was two-story, red brick, with tall, oak entry doors sectioned with leaded glass that reflected the landscape lighting. She'd never considered his financial situation before, but looking at all this, there was no question the man had money.

She turned to look at him, too stunned even to speak.

"Like it?" he asked casually, but she saw the pleasure in his eyes as he watched her.

"It—it's beautiful," she whispered.

"Not too bad for a cowboy." He unbuckled his seat belt. "Come on. I'll show you around."

"Sam. Wait." She touched his arm before he could step out of the truck. "I—I just want to say that, well, today was...nice."

He glanced down at her hand on his arm. "Nice?"

She pulled her hand away, thankful it was dark in the cab so he wouldn't see her blush. "I know it wasn't for real, the ceremony and dinner, but still, I—"

His gaze watched her intently. "You what?"

She closed her eyes, not certain how to explain her feelings, not certain if she wanted to explain them. "This could have been terribly awkward, but you and the Stones made it almost...pleasant."

He raised his brows. "Almost, huh?"

She smiled. "Very pleasant."

Sam had no idea why he suddenly felt a rush of annoyance at her admission. Maybe it was because of the innocence that seemed to shimmer from her, or maybe because of the fact that she looked so damned beautiful at that moment. Or maybe because his gut was twisting from the effort it took to keep from dragging her into his arms, up the stairs and into his bed. He'd show her *very pleasant* and *nice*.

"Well, just consider it a dry run for Ronald, darlin'." He knew the comment was cruel and uncalled for, but his frustration seemed to have control here, not his civility. He leaned close, deepening his voice. "In fact, since he's so understanding, why don't we do a warm-up for the honeymoon while we're at it?"

He hated the words the minute they were out and the hurt in her eyes made him want to kick himself. Dammit! He'd never spoken to a woman that way. He hadn't even realized it was in him until now—until Faith. He didn't like it one little bit.

She slid out of the truck before he could stop her and strode toward the front door with the grace of a queen.

"Faith!" He slammed the truck door behind him, but she didn't stop. He caught up with her in three strides, just before she made it to the door, and took hold of her arm.

The chin was up again, dammit.

"If you'll just show me where my room is, I'll be—"

"Faith—"

"—out of your—"

"Faith!"

Because she wasn't listening, and because she'd pulled away from him, he did the only thing he could think of. He scooped her up in his arms. She gasped as he pulled her tightly against him.

"I'm sorry." When she refused to look at him, he brought his face closer to hers. "You didn't deserve that. It's no excuse, but I'm just edgy, that's all. You can horsewhip me if you like."

She said nothing for a long moment, just sat stiffly in his arms. "I'm really not into that," she said finally, with such a straight face that he wasn't sure if she was kidding. When she smiled softly, he released a long breath.

"I am sorry," he said softly.

She sighed then, wrapped her arms around his neck and looked into his eyes. "Not easy for a confirmed bachelor to take the plunge, is it? Even if it's not for real."

Smiling, he shook his head. "It was nice," he repeated her words. "And very pleasant."

He hadn't even realized that he'd started walking toward the front door—that he was carrying his bride over the threshold. When they stepped inside the entry, he froze.

There were dozens of flickering candles gathered at the base of the sweeping staircase, with pink and ivory rose petals scattered up the steps. On a small entry table beside the stairs, a bottle of opened champagne chilled in a silver bucket beside a vase filled with Old English white roses.

Faith looked at him, her eyes wide. "Did you...?"

He shook his head, wishing he'd thought of it, that he'd been the one to put that look of exquisite pleasure on her face. "Had to be Annie and Jared. They must have come here after they left the restaurant."

The air smelled rose sweet, and the alluring scent of Faith's perfume sent his senses into overdrive. The feel of her warm body against his, her lips softly parted, her slender arms draped around his neck and shoulders....

"Sam," she whispered, "you can put me down now."

He did. Slowly, letting her body slide over his, a

sensuous torture that had him clenching his teeth and swearing silently. Every curve of her body burned him, made his blood boil and his heart pound. Her arms were still around his neck, her eyes half closed, avoiding his gaze as he lowered her to the floor.

He would have made it, he told himself, would have held his control, if only she hadn't looked up at him, her face flushed and her eyes heavy with desire. Her feet never even touched the ground before he covered her mouth with his, slanting his lips against hers, crushing her to him as he deepened the kiss.

Faith had never felt so consumed. Sam's strong arms held her securely, his mouth hard on hers, demanding, insistent. Heat flooded her body, poured through every vein, and because it was impossible not to, she returned his passionate embrace, shuddered from the force stirring in her.

She tightened her arms around his neck, felt his hands cup her bottom and lift her higher, bringing their bodies into a more intimate fit. Her breasts pressed against his hard chest, ached from the need pulsing through her. She wanted his touch on her, his hands, his lips. She made a small, whimpering sound as she felt the pressure from his arousal against her legs, then instinctively and shamelessly moved against him. He moaned, his hands tightening on her, kneading her flesh in his palms.

His lips abandoned hers, and his mouth—hot and wet—dragged over her cheek, her ear. Tasting her, devouring her, it moved lower, to her neck, his tongue swirling over the erratic pulse at the base of her throat. Pleasure swam through her, and the wild sound of her own heart drummed in her head.

"Faith," he whispered hoarsely, and his hot breath seared her skin. "Come with me, upstairs. To my bed."

She heard the raw need in his voice, felt it in her own body. She wanted to. How she wanted to. But what of the morning...what then, after the physical had been sated and she had to face him in the light of day? They were both caught up in the moment, in the day even, but she didn't dare let herself forget that none of this was real. It was all make-believe, a fantasy that would disappear with the rising sun.

The rising sun.

Oh, God, she remembered, closing her eyes. She hadn't told Sam yet about tomorrow. She'd tried—twice—but both times he'd cut her off and refused to listen.

"I—I can't, Sam. I'm sorry." Reluctantly, she eased her body away from his. When her feet touched the floor, her knees barely held her. Stepping away from him, she drew in a shaky breath and leveled her gaze with his.

"Sam, about tomorrow. I—I'm going into the mountains."

The hard set of his face turned to shock. "What the hell are you talking about? I thought we had all that settled."

She shook her head. "No. You had it settled, not me. If I find Digger's body, the estate settlement will go easier and there will be fewer holdups. I need to go, not just for Elijah Jane, but for me, for my mother. I have to know...that...that I at least tried, no matter how futile the attempt may be."

He dragged his hands through his dark hair and

shook his head. "It's insane, Faith. And dangerous. I won't let you do it."

She called every last ounce of resolve and squared her shoulders. "I don't believe you have any choice in the matter, short of tying me up."

"Is that an invitation?" He took a threatening step toward her.

She held her ground, though her stomach did a double flip. "I've already made arrangements. I have a guide arriving here in the morning."

"A guide? Who?"

"I hired him out of a Texas tourist agency. He's trained in mountain backpacking and survival. He came highly recommended."

His eyes were more threatening than the shadows, his face a tight mask of anger. "Highly recommended! By who? Some idiot booking cruises and family vacations to Hawaii? No one knows those mountains well, except Digger and myself."

"You turned me down, Sam. I did what I had to do. I'll be back in a few days and we can complete our two months together as husband and wife." It took all the courage she possessed, but she kept her eyes locked on his. "Now if you'll show me my room, I'd like to go to bed. I have an early day tomorrow."

He took another step toward her, his eyes black with anger. From the intensity of his gaze, she thought he just might be considering getting a rope and tying her up, as she'd so inanely suggested.

"Upstairs," he ground out. "Second door on the left."

She had no idea how she managed to turn on knees

as weak and trembling as hers were, but somehow she did, and even found the strength to walk up the rose-strewn stairs.

She found her room and collapsed on the bed, wondering what the hell she'd gotten herself into.

Five

Faith tiptoed down the stairs the next morning. The large house was quiet, and the gray light of early dawn had just begun to chase the shadows from the corners. The scent of roses filled the cool morning air, and she paused at the foot of the stairs, biting her bottom lip as she stared at the rose petals still strewn about the floor, the melted candles and the untouched bottle of champagne.

She'd never forget the beauty of that moment as they'd stepped through the front door: Sam holding her in his arms, the flickering candles, the sweet scent of roses. Magic, that's what it had been. Enchanting. Seductive.

She'd berated herself half the night for nearly giving in to the illusion, for almost believing herself a new bride with a handsome, virile husband. But under the circumstances, what woman wouldn't have fallen under the spell? What woman wouldn't have imagined herself being carried up those stairs in Sam's strong arms, dreamed of his passionate kisses and his touch as they consummated their vows?

Good grief. She closed her eyes and shook the erotic image out of her mind. Wasn't it bad enough to have fantasized about him all last night, let alone in the light of day? It was nearly six-thirty, and the man she'd hired would be here soon. She had to get her head on straight, keep her attention focused on the matter at hand.

She'd already dressed for her ride into the mountains. Though she'd bought new clothes for the trip and packed the things she was bringing into a large backpack, the blue jeans, blouse and boots that Savannah had given her were most comfortable and she'd decided to wear them today.

She was nervous about the trip, but she had no intention of letting Sam know that. He'd only use it against her, and she refused to be dissuaded by his anger or intimidation. He had no right to issue orders. Even if they were *really* married, which they weren't, she would still never allow a man to boss her about.

Thank goodness Harold was a man of the nineties. He would never try those caveman tactics with her. They would have a logical, open-minded discussion over the issue, exchange opinions—then she would do as she pleased.

Cheered by the prospect of such an open marriage, Faith followed the enticing smell of coffee. Her stomach did a little flip as she reached the kitchen door, but she ignored it. She was going to have to face Sam sometime. Now was as good a time as any.

She stepped into the large, airy kitchen, then placed a hand over her mouth to hold back a gasp. The oak floors and cabinets shone softly; the spotless white-tile counter and center island glistened. Valances of blue gingham hung above the French doors leading to a patio and large swimming pool complete with rock waterfall and tropical greenery. Her apartment in Boston was contemporary design—chrome and marble and straight, simple lines—the complete opposite of the Circle B's country-traditional. She liked this, she realized with surprise. The warm woods, the tall ceilings and large windows. It made her feel comfortable.

Unlike the man who owned it, she mused. He stood at the counter, his back to her as he poured coffee into a mug. She studied him for a moment, watching as he replaced the coffee pot and took a sip from his cup. He wore faded denim jeans and a black T-shirt that accentuated his muscular arms and narrow waist. Power emanated from his long, solid body, power that was as raw as it was sensual. A potent masculinity that caused a shiver to run up her spine.

When he turned and met her eyes with his own, the shiver intensified. He said nothing, just leaned back against the counter, his gaze skimming over her as if he were the cat and she were his breakfast.

"Good morning," she said brightly, determined not to let him know the effect he had on her, or that she'd tossed and turned the entire night.

He nodded.

"Do you mind if I have a cup?" She gestured toward the pot.

"Help yourself." He reached over and opened the cupboard to his left.

He looked tired, she thought, moving toward him. His hair was slightly rumpled, his feet clad only in black socks, and—she swallowed hard—the top snap of his jeans undone. Everything just felt so...intimate.

But she and Sam weren't intimate, she reminded herself. Nor were they going to be. She pulled a mug out of the cupboard, then her heart skipped when he took the cup from her hands, brushing his fingers against hers. The ring on her finger seemed to wink at her, and she pulled her hand quickly away.

"Milk's in the fridge." He filled her mug and handed it back. "Sugar next to the stove."

She spooned sugar into her cup, then filled it with milk. She never used either one; she just needed to keep her hands busy.

"I didn't think I'd see you this morning." She tried the coffee, resisting the urge to wrinkle her nose at the sweetness. "I always thought that ranchers got up with the chickens."

One corner of his mouth lifted. "I'm on my honeymoon."

Dammit, why was he staring at her like that? She felt naked, standing here in the middle of his kitchen, not knowing what to say or do. She held her mug with both hands and took another sip of coffee. "Oh."

"My men won't expect to see me for a while." He watched her over the rim of his cup. "I even gave my housekeeper a few days off. To give me and my wife privacy.''

She couldn't help but wonder what he'd had in mind for those days. Had he, the ultimate bachelor and ladies' man, planned a week's assignation? Her first reaction was a delicious tingling over her skin; the second, irritation at his audacity. ''How thoughtful of you.''

He shrugged. ''Gazella doesn't miss a thing. She'd figure out much too soon that the bride and groom slept in different rooms. I figured it would give us a week to come up with some kind of reason we're not in the same bedroom.''

It made sense, she reasoned, and felt a little guilty—or was it disappointed?—that his intentions hadn't been of a lascivious nature.

''Now all I have to figure out,'' he said dryly, ''is how to explain to my crew why my new wife is going off into the mountains with another man the day after we're married.''

She closed her eyes and groaned softly, thinking of spiders and tangled webs. Because she'd never considered the marriage a real one, it had never occurred to her what his employees might think or how much they knew about his private life.

''Sam—'' she began. The doorbell's deep, musical chime cut her off.

Sam's eyes narrowed as he set his coffee cup down and pushed away from the counter.

''Sam, wait.'' She put a hand on his chest and the heat of his skin even through the thin T-shirt burned her fingers. ''I'm sorry about this. I never intended to embarrass you in front of your men, but there's no other way. We'll think of something, some way to explain this later. But I have to go.''

A muscle jumped at the base of his jaw. ''Do what you have to do.''

She hesitated, then let her hand drop. She almost reached for him again, but he stepped away, turning his back to her as he refilled his cup.

Straightening her shoulders, she drew in a breath and turned. This was how it had to be, she told herself firmly, and headed for the front door. She didn't need Sam McCants to approve of her or what she did. This was *her* business, *her* life, not his.

Sam swore under his breath as the doorbell rang again, then swore again when he overfilled his cup and coffee splashed over the sides. Faith Courtland could do whatever the hell she wanted, he told himself, wiping up the mess with a dishrag. He'd have a few quiet days to himself, catch up on some paperwork, maybe read a couple of those books he'd been meaning to get to. Hell, he might even go fishing. Catch a few of those big trout out of Willoby's Creek. Why not? he convinced himself. He could even camp up there a few days and who would be the wiser that he and Faith weren't together? His crew had all ridden over to the south pasture today. If they didn't see her leave with this guy, whoever the jerk was, Sam just might pull it off.

Warming to the idea, he strolled after Faith, stopping at the kitchen doorway to watch as she opened the front door.

Her ''guide,'' as she'd called him, stepped into the entry, flashing a blinding white smile. Sam told himself that he was being completely objective as he assessed the man: sandy blond hair shaved military-style, bulging biceps under a tight white polo shirt, brand new designer jeans, trendy sunglasses hanging around his neck from a black cord. The only things missing were the photographers from *Weekend Recreational Man* magazine.

"Coleman Bricker," he said loudly, shaking Faith's hand roughly.

Coleman, for God's sake. Sam rolled his eyes. What piece of camping equipment had the guy lifted *that* name from?

Sam frowned when Coleman held onto Faith's hand longer than necessary.

"Mr. Bricker." She pulled her hand away, stepped back to let him in. "Did you have any trouble finding the ranch?"

"Sweetheart, I could have found my way here with my eyes closed in a windstorm." He cocked his head, a practiced gesture, Sam decided irritably. "Don't you worry. You've hired the best with Coleman Bricker. If you lost one of those pretty little fingernails in these mountains, I could sniff it out."

Sam didn't know whether to laugh or groan. Apparently, Faith didn't either. She coughed dryly, then cleared her throat. "That's, uh, terrific. Do you have everything we'll need?"

"Sure do, little lady. Two horses, camping equipment, food. I've studied the maps upside down and inside out and every detail is right here, etched in stone." He pointed to his head.

Etched in nugget, was more like it, Sam thought. A very small nugget, at that.

"Why don't you just call me Faith?" she said

tightly. "I just need to get my things, and I'll be right with you."

Sam's hand tightened around his mug as Bricker watched Faith hurry up the stairs. Sam didn't like this man one little bit, and he especially didn't like him ogling Faith's nicely rounded bottom.

"Hey, there." Sam pushed away from the doorway he'd been leaning against.

Startled, Coleman jumped at Sam's voice. Oh, great, Sam thought. The guy nearly jumps out of his fashion boots at the sound of hello. He couldn't wait to see what Nugget Boy did at the growl of a grizzly or roar of a mountain lion.

"Sam McCants." Sam stuck his hand out. "So you're Faith's mountain man, are you?"

"That's right. Coleman Bricker." He shook Sam's hand.

Bricker's hand was smooth and damp, but his shake was strong, the pressure increasing as a show of machismo. Sam smiled, enjoying the game, and increased his pressure as well. Nugget Boy's face flushed red before he finally pulled away.

Coleman reached into his pocket—with his left hand—and handed Sam a card. "Anything you need. Mountain guide, backpacking, survival weekends. Just give a call."

Sam doubted this guy could survive a mosquito bite, let alone a few days in the mountains. But what business was it of his? he told himself angrily. If the fool woman wanted to waste her time and even get herself killed, that was her problem, not his.

"You familiar with Lonesome Rock Canyon?" Sam asked, sipping his coffee.

"Hell—" Coleman slapped Sam's shoulder "—I know that canyon forward and backward. No need to worry."

"Do I look worried?" Sam glanced at the hand Nugget Boy had left on his shoulder. If that hand wasn't gone in two seconds, Coleman was going to be pulling back a stump.

Enough of a survivalist to know danger when it threatened, Coleman withdrew his hand. "You any relation to Miss Courtland?" he asked carefully.

"Only by marriage," Sam said casually.

"I'm ready."

Faith hesitated halfway down the stairs. She'd pulled her hair into a ponytail, slung her backpack over her shoulder and tied a denim jacket around her waist. And still, Sam thought, she moved down the stairs with the air of a princess.

"I see you two have met." Faith looked steadily at Sam as she stood beside Coleman.

"I've assured Sam here that you're in good hands." Coleman started to slap Sam's shoulder again, then drew back at the glare.

She lifted one eyebrow. "Have you? That was nice of you, Mr. Bricker, but hardly necessary. Was it, Sam?"

"Not necessary at all," Sam agreed.

"Well, ah, we'll be off then," Coleman said after a long, terse moment. "A pleasure, Sam."

Sam just sipped his coffee.

When Coleman finally made his exit, Faith drew in a breath and turned to face Sam. "Well…goodbye."

"Faith—"

Sighing, she closed her eyes. "Sam, please don't try to talk me out of this."

"I wasn't going to."

"Oh." She smiled weakly. "Well, thank you."

He moved toward the stairs, reached down into a box at the foot of the steps. "I didn't think you should leave without this, though."

He pulled out a hat. A black Stetson with a leather band and silver concha. "I thought you'd be needing one around here. I had to guess at the size."

Her lips parted in a soft gasp as he handed her the hat, and slowly, sensuously, she ran her fingers over the smooth fabric, traced the intricate design on the concha. "It's beautiful."

"Go ahead." He smiled. "Put it on."

She did, then moved to the mirror over the entry table and laughed softly at herself. He moved behind her, watched her in the mirror. Damn, but *she* was beautiful.

"It fits." Her eyes were bright with pleasure as she slid her fingers over the brim. She shifted and adjusted the hat until she found just the right angle. Smiling, she looked at him, held his eyes as she whispered, "Thank you."

Did she have any idea how she was looking at him? he wondered. And did she know what that kind of look did to a man? If that idiot she'd hired wasn't waiting right outside, he'd damn well show her. He'd carry her upstairs and make love to her the way he'd wanted to last night, the way he'd wanted to from the moment he'd laid eyes on her.

He stepped away instead, frustrated and furious, not

only with her, but with himself and the entire situation.

Faith took a step toward him. "I—" She stopped suddenly, then sighed. "I'll be back in a few days."

He nodded rigidly, then watched as his *wife* walked out the door with another man.

"To hell with her." He turned sharply and stormed back into the kitchen. "I'm going fishing."

Faith felt certain she'd seen that same crooked pine tree at least three times now. Then there was that rock formation a few yards back shaped like an eagle's head. That had looked alarmingly familiar, too.

Still Coleman, who was riding a few feet ahead of her own chestnut mare, had reassured her that they were right on course, and they would be stopping soon to rest.

She could hardly wait.

Only three hours with this egotistical pretty-boy and already Faith thought she might scream. In fact, if he called her "little lady" one more time, she *would* scream.

That's what she got for hiring the man without an interview first. It served her right, she thought irritably. Even the horses he'd brought were questionable. Her mount was skittish, sidestepping if a leaf blew across her path. If Faith hadn't been raised with horses and competition riding, she'd have landed on her butt long ago. Keeping the horse in line had taken a great deal of concentration and energy, and her arms and thighs were straining from the effort. In spite of her experience with horses, she hadn't ridden in two years. And after an entire day in the saddle with a horse this nervous, there was no question her muscles were going to ache.

But a sore bottom was going to be the least of her concerns, she decided as they rode into a clearing dotted with yellow wildflowers and Texas bluebonnets. A narrow trail ran through the broken tall grass—a trail they'd forged the last time they'd passed through here, which was roughly an hour ago.

Her so-called expert mountain man, backpacker, sniff - out - a - fingernail - and - find - my - way - in - a - windstorm guide was completely and hopelessly lost, she realized.

She'd wanted desperately to back out of this excursion the moment she'd laid eyes on the ridiculous man. She'd seen right through him, of course, but she couldn't bring herself to admit to Sam that he was right, and that she was wrong.

So she'd gone, praying that just maybe Mr. Coleman Bricker would be more professional than peacock, but so far, the only thing the windbag was obviously experienced at was telling stories about himself.

Damn her stubborn pride.

She sighed heavily. She needed to see this through. Whether she found Digger's body or not, whether she proved to herself that he was truly dead or not, she knew she had to try.

Coleman put up a hand, then dismounted a beautiful black gelding who'd been jerking on the reins and throwing his head all morning. "We'll stop... here for...a while."

Coleman's breathing was labored, his face flushed and his white shirt soaked with sweat. *Great,* Faith thought. *The guy will probably pass out and I'll have to go for help.* Sam would get a big kick out of that.

If nothing else, it was a beautiful day. Birds chattered in the pine trees overhead, a breeze rustled the wildflowers, the sky was deep blue.

She pulled her horse beside the gelding, watching her expert guide limp toward a large rock under the shade of a tree.

He sat, then suddenly hollered, jumping up from the rock and waving his arms.

With a loud whinny, Faith's mare reared, while the gelding sidestepped sharply into them. Faith's backpack flew, and she hung onto her saddle with her legs, struggling furiously to control her frightened horse. In two seconds, when the mare's front hooves hit the dirt, Faith knew she was either going to be on her butt, or dashing through brush and branches, out of control. Either way, it was going to hurt.

But the mare didn't bolt. She danced and jerked, but she stayed put. It took a moment for Faith's head to stop spinning and for her to realize why.

Sam.

He stood in front of the mare, tightly holding the reins, speaking calmly to the terrified animal. Coleman's gelding was several feet away, beside three other horses that Sam had obviously brought with him.

Coleman was still dancing as if he had hot coals in his pants.

Faith gathered the reins firmly in her hands. "Sam." She whispered his name as if it were an invocation.

He looked at her, his eyes angry, but asked in a calm voice, ''Are you all right?''

She nodded.

''What the hell is the matter with Nugget Boy over there?'' Sam helped her from the saddle, holding her close as he lowered her to the ground, then gestured to Coleman, who was holding his rear end.

She didn't know why Sam had called the guide that name, but she didn't care, either. It just felt good to have Sam's arms around her. When he released her she reluctantly stepped away. ''I have no idea.''

''A snake,'' Coleman yelled out, pointing toward the rock where he'd been sitting. ''I think a snake bit me.''

Frowning, Sam walked over to the man, then glanced at the rock. ''You sat on a bumblebee,'' he said dryly.

Coleman stilled. ''It felt like a snake,'' he complained.

''Well, it looks like a bumblebee.'' Sam tipped his hat back and inspected the flattened yellow-and-black spot. ''At least, it did.''

Coleman glanced at the smashed insect. His flushed face turned deep red. ''Certainly was a big one, wasn't it?''

Sam said nothing, just stared blandly at the man.

Coleman cleared his throat as he straightened. ''So, Sam, thanks for lending a hand, but everything's fine here now so we'll just be on our way.''

He walked carefully over to his horse and slowly mounted. ''Ah, if you'll just point me in the direction of that canyon, we'll be on our way again.''

Sam walked over to his horses, ignoring a sturdy

roan mare and a large, solid gray. Instead he gathered up the reins of the third horse, a wiry pinto who anxiously tossed his head and pawed at the ground.

Was he really going to leave her with this guy? Faith wondered, and quickly scooped up her backpack. He couldn't, he *wouldn't.* Frantic, she watched as he led the pinto beside Coleman's horse.

"This little horse here knows his way back to the Circle B." Sam dropped the reins. "Just hang on tight and keep your seat."

Coleman frowned at Sam. "I don't know what you're talking about, friend. The little lady and I aren't going back to the Circle B."

"You're half right." Sam tipped his hat back. "The 'little lady,' who just happens to be my wife, is staying here with me."

With a shrill whistle, Sam slapped the pinto on the rear. The horse took off, its hooves throwing dirt, its mane flying. Sam looked at a startled Coleman and grinned. "And you are not."

Coleman's eyes widened as Sam smacked the gelding firmly on the rear end and threw up his hands. The animal bolted, with Coleman hanging on for dear life, his yell echoing from the tops of the pine trees. Faith's horse decided to follow its companion, and took chase.

"And you're not my damn friend," Sam yelled after the retreating horses.

Disbelieving, Faith stared as all three horses and Coleman Bricker disappeared through a grove of trees. Sam, who had collected the roan mare and gray, walked toward her.

"That was terrible." She looked at him. "A horrible thing to do."

"Rotten," he agreed.

She dropped her backpack, closing her eyes as she sat on the ground. He rushed to her side, kneeling beside her as he gathered her in his arms. She pressed her face against the solid security of his chest, relief pumping through her body.

"Faith," he said, his voice hoarse, "honey, are you hurt?"

She started to laugh then, wrapping her arms around his waist. "Bless you," she said between breaths. "Bless you, bless you."

He was surprised by her unexpected display of gratitude. "You aren't mad at me?"

"Mad at you?" She was on the edge of hysteria. "I'm indebted to you for life. You saved me from that pompous windbag."

Shaking his head, he sat beside her in the soft grass and chuckled. She knew she should move away, that he was holding her much too close, that her hands were far too impatient to roam over the hard planes of his chest. Still, she stayed where she was, feeling as if she'd just been rescued from a close encounter with death. And feeling as if an encounter with life—of listening to Sam's heartbeat and feeling his arms around her—was too overwhelming to let go of just yet.

Reluctantly, she eased away from him. "Why did you come?"

"I checked up on Mr. Bricker through a friend of mine who works for the tourist bureau in Midland." His hands lingered on her arms. "Seems that his brother-in-law owns the agency who recommended him, and his certification as a guide is somewhat questionable.''

Her laugh was dry. ''I could have told you that.''

''Why, Faith—'' he said, straightening her hat as he feigned disbelief ''—are you actually admitting that you made a mistake?''

''You warned me against coming up here with the wrong man.'' She lifted her face to look into his eyes, touched his shoulder. ''You're the right man, Sam. You know that you are. Please take me into Lonesome Rock Canyon.''

He stared at her and cursed as he lifted his hat and raked a hand through his hair. ''Woman—'' he said, shaking his head as he settled his hat back on his head ''—you'll be the death of me, yet.''

When he looked down at her lips, she felt the heat of his body seep into hers, felt her own pulse stop, then beat wildly as his hands tightened on her arms....

He released her suddenly and stood, letting her fall backwards. ''Get your backpack on the roan,'' he said, walking away. ''We have to get moving if we're going to make the entrance to the canyon before dark.''

Still trying to catch her breath, she scrambled up after him on legs that felt like warm molasses. ''What about supplies?'' She grabbed her backpack and straightened her hat. ''Coleman had everything on his horse.''

''I've got everything we'll need.'' He mounted his horse and waited for her.

''But how—why would you?'' She tossed her backpack over the mare. ''Unless....''

He grinned at her, then gave his gray a quick jab with his boot heels. The horse galloped easily, in the opposite direction from that which Coleman had been headed.

Mouth open, she stared after him. He had intended to take her all along—before she'd begged him, before she'd admitted that she'd been wrong, and before she told him he was the only man. He'd made her grovel.

Fuming, she jumped in her saddle and rode after him.

Six

The sun had nearly disappeared by the time they reached the mouth of the canyon. Pale light streaked the towering stone walls; starlings chattered; the scent of wild mint carried on the early evening breeze. Postcard pretty now, with the foliage still green from the recent rains, but Sam knew in a few weeks the sun would scorch the rocky terrain. Wildflowers would fade and wither, the shrubbery would turn dry and brown.

He'd needed to push hard all day in order for them to make it this far. The few breaks they'd taken to rest and water the horses had been short, but they'd needed to cover a lot of ground if they were going to stop here, where the shelter of the trees and canyon wall would provide a more secure and comfortable camp for the night.

But getting to the canyon before dark hadn't been his only reason to push hard for the past few hours. He'd needed to work off the tension that had coiled inside him since he'd watched Faith ride off with that idiot this morning. The entire time he'd been packing his bag for his own little excursion to Willoby's Creek, he'd told himself she could do whatever she wanted, that he'd washed his hands of the entire irritating affair. As he'd saddled his horse, he'd felt his anger knotting inside his gut, but still he'd insisted that the woman could do whatever the hell she pleased. She was no concern of his.

But somewhere between his declarations of indifference and complacency, he'd saddled two more horses and, mad as hell, had headed for the mountains.

Damn this woman.

With a heavy sigh, he glanced behind him. Faith rode slumped in her saddle, obviously exhausted, but when she saw him turn and look at her, she straightened immediately.

"We'll stop here." He pointed to the thicket of oaks, and when they pulled under the canopy of thick branches he slid off his horse.

"Need some help?" he offered when she stayed in her saddle.

"Not at all." Her shoulders squared. "I'm just... looking around for a moment."

He smiled up at her. "Can't move, can you?"

She stared straight ahead. "Not even a toe."

Because he thought it might not be a good idea to laugh at the moment, he simply moved beside her and took hold of her waist. She braced her hands on his shoulders and slid sideways into his arms. He lowered her carefully and when her feet touched the ground, she dropped her hands from his shoulders. "You can let go now," she said primly.

"You sure?"

"Of course, I'm sure."

He shrugged and released her.

She uttered a little shriek when her knees gave out under her, and quickly reached for him again.

"All right." She clutched his arms. "Maybe I do need a minute or two. And you needn't look so damn smug. I haven't ridden for a while, that's all. I'm a little rusty."

Damn but she was pretty when her cheeks turned pink and that cute little chin of hers lifted. He resisted the urge to nuzzle her soft neck, knowing that his advances would be far from welcome at the moment. He chose another, more advantageous tactic. "You handled that little chestnut well this morning. A less experienced rider would have been airborne."

"A compliment, Mr. McCants?" Her tone was cool, but pleasure warmed her blue eyes. "We both know that if it hadn't been for you, Mr. Bricker and I would still be walking—make that limping—back to the ranch right now. Providing my 'expert guide' could have found his way."

The image of Faith's horse rearing as he'd ridden into the clearing, and what might have happened if he hadn't shown up when he had, sent a fresh wave of anger coursing through Sam. But there was another emotion, one he wasn't certain how to deal with: fear. A panic that had knifed through him, sharp and deep. If Faith had been hurt—even a bruise—bumblebees and runaway horses would have been the least of Nugget Boy's troubles.

Realizing that his hands had tightened on Faith's arms, he released her. She wobbled backward, still unsteady on her feet, but he resisted the urge to reach for her again. His emotions were churning right now, on edge, and if he touched her again, he wasn't certain what he might do.

"I'm going to set up camp and get a fire started. You think you can manage the horses?"

"Yes, sir, Captain." She gave a snappy salute. "Right away."

Frowning, he turned sharply and walked away, leaving Faith to wonder if she would ever understand this man's moods. One minute he was charming and gentle, like he had been when he'd given her the hat; the next minute he was a grouchy bear barking orders, like right now. Whoever said women were fickle had obviously never met Sam McCants.

By the time she'd tended to the horses and unloaded her backpack, the woodsy scent of Sam's campfire filled the night air. She noticed that he'd also swept clean a patch of grass under the gnarled branch of an oak and set up two sleeping bags. She stared at the bedrolls laying side by side, then looked at Sam, who knelt beside the fire, feeding the flames with kindling.

Suddenly the relief she'd felt over Sam's rescue turned to uncertainty. She hadn't really thought about the sleeping arrangements. Under the stars, surrounded by nature, just the two of them....

"Something wrong?"

Startled by his question, she glanced up sharply,

clutching her backpack tightly to her. "Wrong?" Annoyed at the catch in her voice, she cleared her throat. "What could possibly be wrong?"

He followed the direction of her gaze, then looked back at her, smiling slowly. "Why, Faith, darlin', don't tell me you're worried about being alone with me."

"Of course I'm not," she lied. "I was just thinking about...insects."

He raised one brow. "Six-legged or two?"

She shrugged, holding back the impulse to smile, then moved beside him. Her legs and arms ached from riding all day, her bottom hurt and her feet were swollen. Slowly, cautiously, she sank down in front of the fire, groaning when her rear end made contact with the hard ground. "I'm still not sure I forgive you for letting me go on this morning, making me beg you to take me into the canyon, when you'd already decided to bring me."

"Oh, that." Sam hoped she couldn't see the twitch at the corner of his mouth. "It hardly seemed polite to interrupt you, you being so intent and all."

"Polite? Ha! You were rubbing my nose in it, McCants, and you know it. It wasn't enough for me to admit I'd made a mistake with that jerk. You wanted to see me crawl and kiss your boots."

Not exactly what he'd had in mind, Sam thought, remembering the feel of her hands on his chest as he'd held her in his arms, and the soft sound of her voice when she'd asked him to take her into the canyon. She'd had a vulnerable look. The desire to make love to her right there, to pull her under him, with the grass as their blanket and the sky their ceiling, had been overwhelming. It had taken every ounce of willpower he possessed to let her go—but he had. A bit roughly, perhaps, but the raw need burning in him had felt anything but gentle.

Needing a distraction from his thoughts, he pulled a can of beef stew and a small cooking pan out of his backpack. He noticed Faith bite her bottom lip as he opened the can and dumped the contents into the pan. They'd had sandwiches earlier, when they'd stopped to rest and water the horses around noon, but nothing since then. Based on his own appetite, and the look in her eyes as she stared at the stew, he was certain she was starving.

Next he pulled out a soft French roll, one of the dozen he'd tossed into his backpack that morning. "Forgive me now?" he asked, handing her the roll.

She hesitated, then gingerly took the bread with a toss of her blond head and a murmur of thanks. In spite of her hunger, she munched daintily, watching him while he heated up the stew. Her eyes glowed soft blue in the light of the fire, and her hair shone with highlights of red and gold. Several silken curls had escaped from her ponytail, framing her delicate face, and Sam felt his throat contract just looking at her.

"How did you find us this morning?" she asked after a moment.

"Wasn't hard." He grabbed a roll himself, trying his damnedest to keep his eyes off those soft lips nibbling a piece of bread. "You were traveling in circles around Madman's Meadow."

"Madman's Meadow?"

"It's an intricate labyrinth of trails that crisscross

through the trees, eventually leading back to the meadow unless you know the right path. Digger taught Jake and me every rock and tree when we were twelve."

She seemed to study the roll in her hand, then asked softly, "What was he...Digger, like?"

Sam pushed three red-hot stones out of the fire with a piece of wood, then set the pan of stew on them. "Everything you've heard so far—cantankerous, ornery, stubborn. Definitely opinionated. But underneath all that grit and mettle, he was kind and compassionate. No one out of work in this town ever paid a penny in his restaurant. If they had a family, he'd send a truckload of food, complaining he'd overbought and hadn't the room to store it. There wasn't a fund-raising in Cactus Flat that he didn't support or a work party where he didn't lend a hand. He was a man of his word, honest, hardworking and fair."

The air had turned cool; the moon rose full and bright over the canyon walls. Faith stared into the flickering flames, her lips pressed tightly together.

"Honest?" she repeated harshly. "A man of his word? Is that what you call a man who abandons the woman carrying his child?"

Sam shook his head. "I don't know what your mother told you, but that's not the Digger I knew."

"What my mother told me—" she looked at him, her eyes bright "—was that her father refused his consent, argued that Digger was too old for her, a drifter and an opportunist who wanted to cash in on the Buchanan money. Digger had left her in Boston, gone back to Texas, supposedly to buy land for a ranch. He was going to send for her as soon as a house was built.''

''That twenty-thousand acres was for your mother,'' Sam said thoughtfully, then frowned. ''Are you saying that he never sent for her?''

The emotion Faith had shown him only a moment ago was under control now, Sam noted. Her voice was calm. ''My mother told me she sent Digger a letter, telling him she was pregnant, that they needed to marry right away. My grandfather intercepted the letter, then told her that Digger had been paid off, that he was never coming back. At the same time, they told Digger that my mother wanted nothing to do with him, that he was a fool to think that a poor miner and cook could ever have made her happy, and she was going to marry someone else. Two weeks later she married my father, Joseph Courtland III, ensuring a merger between Courtland Investments and Buchanan, Fitz and Roy.''

''Their marriage was a business merger?'' Sam asked in astonishment.

''They each had something to gain. My mother, a name for her unborn child, my father, more power and prestige. They stayed together for twenty-six years, until my father's death. A paragon of Boston society, the perfect family.'' She tossed a twig into the fire, watched it shrivel up and disappear. ''Never mind they slept in separate bedrooms and never loved each other.''

''Sounds like us.''

She glanced up, her eyes like blue ice. ''There's no child involved between us, no one we'll be lying to for twenty-six years. In two months, you'll go your way and I'll go mine. No one will be hurt.''

He'd hit a nerve. ''The truth was tough, wasn't it? Finding out about your parents, about Digger?''

''No one likes to find out that their life was a lie.'' She shrugged. ''Whatever happened in the past is unimportant now. What *is* important is Elijah Jane. I'll do whatever I need to do in order to hold it together, to keep it strong.''

''Are you sure you're talking about Elijah Jane?'' he asked. ''Or yourself?''

He could see her first instinct was to argue. She even opened her mouth to do so, then sighed and leaned back on her elbow. ''Okay, so I admit I like my life in order. I also admit I like being in the driver's seat, knowing where I am and where I'm going. Is there anything wrong with that?''

He dug a fork out of his backpack. ''Depends on how much of the scenery you miss while you're staring straight ahead. Here, have a bite.''

She obliged him, then gave a small groan of appreciation. ''Hmm. I do love a man who cooks.''

Sam took a bite, as well, but found more pleasure watching Faith enjoy her food. ''What about Arnold?''

''Of course I love Arnold,'' she said quickly—a little too quickly—then frowned. *''Harold.''*

Smiling, Sam scooped up another bite. ''I mean, does he cook?''

''Well, I—'' she furrowed her brow ''—well, of course he cooks. He's a wonderful cook.''

''You're a terrible liar, Faith.'' Sam shook his head

with disapproval, then offered her another forkful of stew. "Just how well do you know this guy?"

"We eat out a lot." She leaned closer to accept the bite, then scowled and took the plate and fork from him. "And I've known Harold for years. He's an accountant with his father's law firm. We belong to the same gym, have the same friends. We even like the same movies."

He rolled his eyes. "Sounds like you're real pals."

Faith speared a carrot and waved it at Sam. "As a matter of fact, we are. It's important to make sure that two people are compatible before they get married, you know. And if a relationship is going to last, it has to be based on mutual trust and honesty."

Sam reached out and held Faith's fingers still, then bit the carrot off the fork. He chewed slowly, watching her eyes widen and her lips part softly as he continued to hold her hand. He leaned closer, until their shoulders were touching and his face was only inches away from hers. "What about sex, darlin'?"

Faith wasn't certain if Sam's question was an invitation or an inquiry about Harold, but his low, husky voice so close to her ear flowed through her veins as if it were a rich, red wine. Intoxicated by his closeness, by the masculine scent of man and leather and animal, her mind reeled.

"Sex?" she repeated, amazed at the throaty, sensual tone she heard in her own voice. His thumb was making erotic circles on the back of her hand, and the rough texture of his skin sent ripples of electricity up her arm.

"Yeah. Sex." His hot whisper fanned her ear. He slid the fork from her limp fingers, then the plate.

"Don't you think that compatibility in sex is important in a relationship?"

She had no voice; she simply nodded.

His lips skimmed her ear, her cheek. "But not just any sex," he said hoarsely. "I'm talking about the real thing. Wild, furious, raw sex. Can't breathe, can't think, hot sex."

She couldn't breathe or think at the moment. And she was definitely hot. His mouth moved lighter than a feather over her lips. She closed her eyes… waiting…

Nothing.

She opened her eyes slowly, confused at the sudden cold that had settled over her. Sam sat watching her, the plate of stew in one hand, fork in the other. He smiled at her.

Damn him.

He sat there looking so smug, it was all she could do not to smash that plate of stew over his head. He'd rattled her to the core and he knew it. This was all a big game to him.

Well, fine, then. Two could play just as easily as one.

She groaned loudly and grabbed her leg.

He set the plate down and leaned over her. "What's wrong?"

"Cramp," she gasped from between clenched teeth. "Pain. Terrible."

"Where?" Worry etched his brow. "Your leg?"

"My calf!"

He grabbed hold of her calf and started to rub. "Better?"

"Nooo," she moaned.

He moved between her legs, massaging the calf she'd been pointing at. She sat back on her elbows, watching him work, impressed with the gentle but thorough stroke of his hands as he kneaded her leg. She moaned again, though not intentionally this time, enjoying the pleasure that radiated upward from his touch.

It was hard to pinpoint the exact moment the worry on his face turned to something else...something sensual. His hands moved over her leg; then his gaze skimmed up her thigh, to the juncture of her legs, over her belly, across her breasts. And when his eyes finally met hers, the hunger she saw there, the intensity, nearly took her breath away.

They stared at each other, his face like granite in the flickering light of the fire. He knelt between her legs, his large, muscular body towering over her like some mythical Greek god, ready to take what belonged to him.

Her heart slammed in her chest. What a fool she'd been to think she could best him at this game. An absolute fool.

His hands tightened almost painfully on her leg, but still, pleasure pulsed through her veins. The temptation to draw him to her, to wrap her legs around his waist and pull him close, nearly overwhelmed her.

But logic and reason had been her taskmasters for too many years. Sam McCants was not in her plans, or in her future. If she couldn't control her feelings now, how would she manage to survive the next two months?

"Thanks." She pulled her leg from his hands and sat, stretching casually, though her insides were shaking. "It's much better now. I think I'll go walk it off."

She stood slowly, avoiding his gaze as she limped off, knowing that if she looked back, she just might throw herself into his arms and beg him to take her right there, right then, reason and logic be damned.

It was barely dawn when Sam woke to the flutter of wings from a nearby dogwood and the sound of the creek rushing in the gully below. And despite the fact that his neck had a kink, his left arm had fallen asleep, and a rock stabbed his lower back, he couldn't remember a more pleasant awakening.

When they'd gone to sleep last night, Faith's sleeping bag had been at least three feet from his. Now, she was all but sleeping on top of him, with her bag snuggled against his and her body curled up beside him like a ribbon on a present.

And it wasn't even his birthday, he thought with a smile.

Careful not to disturb her peaceful slumber, he glanced over his shoulder. Her head was nearly buried in his shoulder, her tousled hair covering her face. Even through the sleeping bags, he felt the soft contours of her body pressed against his: her breasts tantalizing against his back, her stomach enticing against his rear and those long, long legs of hers molding to his.

Damn.

He counted to ten, preparing to wake her. He had only reached eight when she snuggled closer yet and sighed against his neck.

Damn. Damn. Damn.

He gritted his teeth. Hadn't last night been torture enough? All that talk about sex and compatibility, about Faith's fiancé and what buddies they were. Lord knew he'd wanted to kiss her senseless right then and there, just to see if he could make her forget the guy's name.

He still wanted to kiss her senseless.

She made a soft, mewing sound and rubbed her legs against his.

He swore. He'd been so damn proud of himself last night, too. That he'd actually found the willpower to resist those tempting lips, that he'd turned her cool, calm, collected routine right back at her.

Then she had to go and get a leg cramp, of all things. It had been bad enough, rubbing her calf, kneeling between her legs, but when he'd looked down at her, lying on the ground underneath him, with the firelight dancing in her blond hair and her blue eyes soft and bewitching, he'd felt himself falling right over the edge.

If she hadn't pulled away as quickly as she had and walked off, there was no doubt in his mind where they would have ended up: in one sleeping bag, naked.

Exactly where he'd wanted to be.

There'd been little conversation between them after that aside from a few curt questions and replies. Then they'd each climbed into their own separate sleeping bags several feet apart, backs to each other, and said good-night.

And now here they were, wrapped around each other like strands in a braid. He looked over his shoulder. At least, Faith was wrapped around him, he thought, as much to his pleasure as to his discomfort.

He could just move away, carefully ease himself out. Then she'd never be the wiser and she wouldn't have to be embarrassed.

Nah. He smiled slowly. That wouldn't be any fun.

He rolled onto his back and slipped an arm under her head, regretting that the sleeping bags still separated them. She mumbled something, then nestled closer, burrowing her cheek against his chest.

''Morning, darlin',' ' he whispered.

''Hmm,'' she replied, moving against him, a slow, sensuous slide of her body over his.

Camping out would never be the same again, Sam thought, biting back a groan. And as much as he would have liked to continue their ''conversation,'' he didn't think his resistance could stand much more of her snuggling. Her hand was splayed on his chest, her fingers moving caressingly back and forth.

''You keep doing that, darlin',' ' he drawled, ''and you're going to have company in that sleeping bag before you can shake a shoulder.''

Her hand stilled, then her entire body. Keeping her head down, she inched away, then disappeared into her sleeping bag.

Laughing, he bent over her. ''You should've warned me you're so amorous in the morning, Faith. I would have zipped my bag.''

''Go away.'' She kicked a leg out at him, at least, he thought it was a leg, and huddled deeper into her covers.

He placed an elbow on the rounded form protruding from the center of her sleeping bag. She tried to wiggle away, but he leaned his weight against her, trapping her inside her cocoon.

"Don't you worry none, sweetheart." He patted her bottom. "Your secret's safe with me."

She wiggled out from under him and stuck her head out of the bag. Her hair was wild and tousled, her face flushed. He grinned at her.

"I was not being amorous," she snapped, combing her fingers through her hair. "I was cold. And I was asleep. You took advantage of me."

"I took advantage of you?" He gave a snort of laughter. "Darlin', I thought I'd woke up with an octopus wrapped around me. Oh, no, you don't—" he said as she reached for a boot to throw at him "—you start throwing things and I might not take you to the hot springs today."

She dropped the boot, then blew the bangs out of her eyes and sat up straighter. "Hot springs?"

"I thought that might get your attention." He grinned at her. "It's kind of a pretty little spot right next to the river about halfway down the canyon. Just like bathwater."

"Bath?" She said the word reverently and hugged her sleeping bag.

"If we make good time today, we could camp there for the night, even." He stretched casually and lay back down.

"Oh, no, you don't." She grabbed the edge of his sleeping bag and pulled, rolling him out onto the ground. "Get your butt moving, McCants. The day's a-wasting."

Sam McCants belonged on a horse. He rode as if he'd been born to ride, as if it came as naturally to him as breathing. His tall, work-honed body fit into a saddle like that of no man Faith had ever seen before. His shoulders were broad, his arms solid muscle and his hands—she noticed, watching him guide his horse through a thicket—were large and strong. Hands that demanded attention and commanded respect.

And yet they were gentle hands, as well, she knew.

With the sun warm overhead and bright yellow butterflies swirling around the purple wildflowers, Faith let her mind wander. She thought of those hands, how he'd held her at the base of the stairs the night they were married, how he'd kissed her, touched her, made her bones feel weak and her heart pound…how he could have carried her up those stairs, to his bed…how she'd wanted him to….

Her horse stumbled on a rock and she gasped, nearly falling from her saddle from the unexpected jolt. She grabbed for the reins as the animal righted herself.

"Problem?" Sam looked over his shoulder.

"I'm fine." *I was just daydreaming about you and almost fell on my butt, that's all.* "No problem."

He eyed her suspiciously. "Would you tell me if there was?"

"Of course I would." She smiled sweetly.

It was a lie, and they both knew it. But there was no way she was going to let him think that she couldn't keep up, or that she wasn't tough enough to cut the mustard. She *was* tough enough. And she *could* keep up.

So she got a little cold last night and had moved

in closer to him. Even through his sleeping bag the man radiated like a furnace. Why shouldn't she take advantage of a little body heat? And there'd certainly been plenty of that when she'd woken and found herself in his arms. Her insides still felt warm every time she thought about it.

Which was too damn often.

He'd had a smug smile all day, during their breakfast of yummy granola bars and dried fruit, through two miles of steep, downward riding on narrow trails, and through their taste-tempting lunch of dried jerky and trail mix. She just knew he was waiting for her to complain so he could drag her back.

Well, she wasn't going to complain, and she wasn't going to let him take her back. She'd come this far, and she would go the distance, no matter what. And tonight she would make certain that her sleeping bag wasn't anywhere near Sam McCants's. She would freeze before she made that mistake again.

Sam stopped his horse and pointed beyond a tall outcrop of rocks, beyond the tree tops, to where steam billowed high in the air.

He turned in his saddle and grinned at her. "Your bath awaits, m'lady."

After two days of riding in warm weather, Faith needed no encouragement. The trail narrowed under a canopy of cottonwood trees, then descended sharply between steep walls of rugged rock. When they reemerged into the open, Faith felt her breath catch in her throat.

A waterfall cascaded behind a pool of steaming water. Ferns spilled from rocks and boulders; masses of tiny white flowers sweetly scented the air. Trees and bushes were alive with birdsong and butterflies. And beside all the lush, calm beauty, the canyon river surged and roared, like a golden lion ready to climb the banks of its cage and swallow the prized bird.

Pretty? Sam had called this place? She looked at him, saw the pleasure in his eyes as he watched her.

"Like it?" he asked.

"It's beautiful," she breathed.

"I'll set up camp here." He dismounted behind an embankment of boulders, then reached up to help her off her horse. "The river's still high and rough, but there's a few feet of rocks between the current and the hot springs. Just keep away from the rapids and you can go play to your heart's content."

Go play? She laughed at his expression. The word play hadn't been in her vocabulary for years. She wasn't sure it ever had been. But suddenly she wanted to. She wanted to skip and kick up her heels, and whatever else people did when they played. But the old Faith clucked her tongue, reminding her that this was no vacation, that this was a serious expedition—they were looking for a *body* for heaven's sake. They were searching for the man who had been her father.

Her smile faded before her feet touched the ground. She wasn't here to have fun, or to enjoy herself. What was the matter with her? How could she have forgotten herself like that?

"Uh, oh. I recognize that look." Sam cupped her chin in his hand. "Taskmasters aren't allowed here, sweetheart."

"But—"

"We're stopping for the night anyway," he cut her off. "There'll be plenty of time later to think about responsibility and duty. Right now, just let yourself go with it, Faith. Enjoy."

His fingers moved over her jaw, and his touch warmed her. Whoever said reality wasn't as good as fantasy had never met Sam McCants. Here she was, alone with a sexy, handsome man, in a secluded lush paradise, and all she had to do was enjoy herself. Excitement and pleasure bubbled up in her at the thought, mingling with the thrilling touch of his hand on her skin. She could give in to the feeling now, she realized. She could invite him to join her. They could both...enjoy.

She looked into his eyes. They weren't smiling now. They were wild, exciting. She wanted this man—wanted to feel his hands and his mouth, on her skin, everywhere, all at once. She wanted more than she'd ever wanted before.

And then it crept in, stronger than any emotion she'd ever felt. Fear. Not of him, but of herself, of what she stood to lose with this man. And that was what made her take a deep breath, then step away.

She reached for her backpack, forcing her hands not to shake, forcing a light tone. "Since there're no locks on the doors, Mr. McCants, I expect you to be a gentleman."

He tipped his hat back and smiled, a slow, rakish grin that brought flutters to her stomach. "You expect a lot from a guy, Faith."

She tossed her backpack over her shoulder. "Never more than I'd give in return, cowboy. When it's your turn, I promise not to look, either."

"I don't mind," he called after her, but she merely waved.

She set out a fresh change of clothes and a towel on a boulder beside the hot springs, then quickly pulled her clothes and hat off, leaving only her underwear for modesty's sake. When she dipped her foot into the pool, she sighed with delight.

The water was heavenly. Bubbling and hot. She walked in cautiously, making certain she had a good foothold on the sand and rocks. She'd never live it down if she had to call Sam because she broke her leg wading into a pool of water. Not to mention having him see her in her state of undress.

It wasn't deep, maybe five feet at the most in some areas. She swam, letting the water take the dust and sweat and grime from her skin. Looking at the sky overhead and the waterfall cascading down the rocks into the pool, she couldn't remember when she'd ever felt so relaxed, so free. She'd never taken time for vacations, she'd always enjoyed her work too much to take time off. Maybe she had been missing something, she decided. Maybe she would call a travel agent when she got back home—look into a cruise, or Hawaii or the Caribbean.

But she had the wedding to deal with when she returned to Boston. And there'd be so much work to catch up with. Board meetings, project dates to complete, a restructuring of management. There'd be no time for a vacation.

No, she thought with a sigh—floating in the water, feeling the aches and pains of two days' riding in the saddle ease from her body—she'd have to be content with these few hours here, in this place. She consoled herself with the fact that she and Harold were supposed to go on a honeymoon in a few months. Maybe they'd go somewhere tropical. She forced herself to smell the coconuts, hear the island music as she lay on the warm sand, soaking up the sun, her husband's large, strong hands rubbing suntan lotion on her back, massaging her shoulders, her arms, running his fingers sensuously over her heated skin....

But something was wrong, she realized. Harold didn't have large, strong hands. Frowning, she turned in her daydream to the man caressing her skin and looked up into his dark eyes.

Harold didn't have dark eyes, either. It wasn't Harold.

It was Sam.

She opened her eyes with a start, annoyed that he intruded on her thoughts everywhere. Even on her honeymoon!

Irritated, she pulled herself from the water onto a large boulder, shaking the water out of her hair and Sam McCants out of her mind. Two feet below her, on the other side of the boulder, the river raged, spraying cold, frothy water on her back.

Her skin was burning, her insides hot and jumbled. Coming out of the pool, the river water felt wonderfully cooling. She reached out, scooped the cold water in her hands and splashed her face. Much better, she decided, surprised that cold water did indeed cool the fire pumping through her body.

She reached out once more...just one more scoop...then slipped on the moss-covered rock and fell into the rushing river.

Seven

Sam had been thinking about a cold shower when Faith's scream ripped through the late afternoon air. The sound of her humming and splashing only a minute before had been like bamboo under his fingernails, and the image of her frolicking naked in the pool was making his blood boil.

Now, her scream turned his insides to ice.

He dropped the wood he'd been collecting and spun in the direction of the pool. She wasn't there. He yelled for her, listened, then called her name again.

The river!

Frantic, he raced to the edge of the boulders, desperately searching for her, calling to her. He scanned the shoreline, but all he saw was river, whitecapped and angry.

"Faith!"

He heard his name then, as a faint shriek downstream. He scrambled along the bank, struggling in the damp, soft dirt to gain a foothold. Shrub and low tree branches slowed him, but he fought his way down an incline to a bend in the river, following the sound of Faith's voice and calling back to her.

There! He spotted her, not four feet from shore, clinging to a rock, fighting to keep her head above water. The river raged around her, threatened to pull her under. He sprinted to the edge of the shore, grabbed a cottonwood branch hanging low over the water. "Grab hold," he yelled, reaching out to her.

"Sam!" She stretched one hand out. He strained to get closer to her, praying that the branch he held on to wouldn't break and send him tumbling into the current.

Her fingers were only inches from him when the river swept her up, then swallowed her.

He leaped in after her.

She reappeared, sputtering, three feet away from him and he lunged for her, grabbing hold of her waist as the current played tug-of-war.

"Hold on to me," he ordered. Her arms were limp as she slid them around his neck. *"Tighter."*

The river dragged them along effortlessly, as if they were toys on a string. Sam didn't bother to fight it; the effort would only have spent valuable energy. They hadn't much time before the river turned again, became deeper and swifter. He had to get them out now.

He saw his chance maybe twenty yards ahead. A small dam of logs and branches caught on some rocks. If he could grab hold of a branch and it didn't break loose from the rocks, they just might be able to work their way to shore.

Ten yards. The current whipped them to the left, just out of reach.

Faith screamed at the sudden tug and one of her arms slipped away.

"You hang on to me, dammit," he barked at her. "Show me what the real Faith Courtland is made of."

It was all the challenge she needed. Both of her arms clamped firmly around his neck. Her chin, though shaking and slightly blue, lifted.

Two yards.

"Here we go..." He kicked with all his strength and leaped across the current, hating that he had to let go of Faith to grab on to the branch protruding from the stockpile of river debris. He grasped the branch firmly in his hands, felt it give way under the weight of their bodies. He pulled hard, swinging them into the pile of twigs and wood caught on the rocks. The branch he held broke loose, but he lunged for another branch and that one held.

Still fighting the current, he inched his way across the dam into shallow water, then dragged them both from the frigid water. They collapsed onto the shore, choking and coughing. He wanted to kiss the wet ground. He wanted to kiss Faith.

But first he had to get her back to camp, get her warm. Her skin felt icy, her teeth were chattering, and she was shaking like a leaf, a combination of fear and cold. And those two little strips of wet, white lace she wore certainly were no help.

He scooped her up, impulsively dropped a kiss on

her shivering mouth, and covered the ground back to camp like a man possessed. "The hot springs will warm you up," he suggested, but she shook her head.

"No more water for now," she whispered, burrowing her head against his shoulder, trembling helplessly. "Just my clothes."

He grabbed a blanket from his backpack instead, and covered her with them as he set her down on a soft mound of grass. He had a fire blazing within three minutes. Eyes closed, she leaned toward it.

He knelt beside her, pushed her dripping hair from her face.

"Are you hurt?"

She opened her eyes slowly, looking at him as if she'd just woken from a nightmare. "You're all wet."

He smiled at her. "A swim in the river with your clothes on does that."

She blinked, staring at him with an intensity that made his pulse quicken. "You could have died."

He didn't want to remind her that it was she who had almost died, too. He didn't even want to think about it. "Die on my honeymoon? Not a chance, Mrs. McCants. You aren't going to get rid of me that easy."

She started to reach out to him, then pulled her shaking hand back and hugged the blanket more tightly around her. "I slipped on a rock," she whispered roughly. "Sam, I'm so sorry."

Sorry? All he wanted to do was enclose her in his arms, pull her inside of him, and she was apologizing? He didn't want her gratitude, dammit. He wanted *her.* With a desperation that even he didn't understand.

But already she was pulling away from him. Drawing back, filing all her emotions into straight little rows, like soldiers at attention. He wanted to shake her, but she was still trembling, still pale, and he didn't trust himself to touch her right now.

He tossed her a towel, then stood and stripped off his shirt and boots. She glanced quickly away and busied herself drying her hair with the towel. He didn't give a damn if he was embarrassing her. He was cold, the fire was warm, and he wasn't going to go strip out of his wet clothes behind some tree because she was modest.

She'd almost died, dammit. The image of her disappearing under the current hit him like an electric shock. He tried not to think what might have happened if he hadn't reached her in time...if the river had taken her, as it had taken Digger.

"You have every right to be angry with me." She sniffed, then sat up and offered him the towel. "My carelessness could have gotten you killed. It's unforgivable."

"Damn straight." He snatched the towel from her, dragged it over his head and chest. "See that it doesn't happen again."

She shook her head. "It won't. It was a mistake, the worst kind. I'll pay much closer attention next time you tell me to do something."

"Good." He threw the towel back at her. "Then listen to this. Shut up, Faith."

Eyes wide, she stared at him. "Excuse me?"

"I said shut up. As in close your trap, be quiet, muzzle it."

"You *are* angry with me."

"Yes, dammit." He spun away, raking his tense hands through his damp hair. How could she be so controlled, so calm? "But not because you made a mistake and fell in the river, and certainly not because you didn't listen to me."

Needing to work off the adrenaline still pumping through his body, he paced. "If I hadn't heard your scream, if that rock hadn't slowed you down or if you'd been even six more feet out, you'd be gone."

She sat rigid, her face ashen in the firelight. "But you did hear me, and I'm not gone. I'm here. And I'm fine."

"How can you be fine?" He whirled on her, his hands clenched into fists. "I watched that river swallow you, take you under. I never felt so helpless, so completely impotent in my life. So don't tell me you're *fine,* dammit, because I'm not. You almost *died,* Faith. Don't you realize that?"

"Yes, I do."

Her words were no more than a whisper, barely audible. In his own anger, his own frustration, he hadn't really looked at her. But the quiver in her voice, the quiet distress, caught his attention and he looked at her now. Her face was deathly pale, her cheeks glistening with tears.

Muttering an oath, he knelt down beside her and gathered her in his arms. "Oh, baby. I'm sorry, I'm sorry. I shouldn't be yelling. I'm just crazy right now, that's all. I almost lost you."

She trembled uncontrollably, but it was the helpless

sobbing that tore at his gut. Dammit, he was such an idiot. She'd almost died and he starts shouting at her because she was trying to be brave. He pulled her onto his lap and held her tightly, struggling to deal with his own raging emotions.

Darkness moved in behind the setting sun, the fire danced and crackled, and still he held her, murmuring sweet words, rocking her in his arms, brushing his mouth over her temple. She stilled finally, then breathed a deep, shuddering sigh against his shoulder.

"Better?" he asked.

Nodding, she cuddled closer, laying her palms on his chest.

"You don't have to be strong all the time, Faith." Her fingers were warm now, he noted. Very warm. And soft, too.

"You're right," she said softly.

"It's all right to let go once in a while." The last word caught in his throat as she pressed her mouth to his shoulder.

"Okay."

Her hands started moving sensuously over his chest. Her teeth nibbled his neck.

"Faith," he choked out. "What are you doing?"

She lifted her mouth to his. "I'm letting loose, Sam."

"Good Lord, I didn't mean to let go like that."

If the situation had been different, Faith might have laughed at the shocked tone in Sam's voice. Heaven knows, she was shocked herself. It wasn't every day she threw herself at a man. In fact, there'd never been *any* day she'd thrown herself at a man.

But she didn't feel like laughing right now. She felt something entirely different.

She understood how close she'd come to death, and with that understanding came an incredible calm—a confidence to listen to her heart, to set aside pretense, to relinquish control and to let herself feel.

She ran her fingertips over the muscles in his shoulders, felt him tense under her touch. How long had she wanted to do that? How long had she fantasized about it? Too long.

A lifetime.

He took hold of her wrists, eased her away. "Sweetheart, you've had a bad experience."

"That's right. I almost died," she reminded him softly, then leaned into him and pressed her lips where her fingers had been only a moment before.

He sucked in a breath, let it out again. "You aren't thinking clearly."

"I've never thought more clearly in my life."

The blanket slipped from her shoulders, and he let go of her wrists to grab for it. She took advantage of the freedom and fanned her palms on his chest, thrilled at the play of hard muscle and dark crisp hair under her fingers. She felt the heavy pounding of his heart.

"Faith, honey—" he said as he replaced the blanket snugly around her shoulders "—you're making it awful hard for me...I mean, to be a gentleman."

"Don't you know a gentleman never refuses a lady?" she purred. Her lips moved upward to his neck, then to his strong jaw—a jaw tightly clenched at that moment. "You're so tense. Come closer and I'll relax you."

"No, you need—"

"You." She pulled his head toward her, his mouth down to hers. "I need you."

He smelled and tasted like the river. Wild. Wet. Untamed. His hands tightened on her shoulders, neither pulling her toward him nor pushing her away.

She knew it was more than her fall in the river that made her so bold. The primitive setting; the two of them alone in the mountains; civilization miles and miles away. But it didn't matter. Only *this* mattered. Instinct was all she had to go on. She let it guide her, reassure her.

His lips were stiff against hers, his strong body tightly coiled, but she felt the need vibrate from his lips into hers. She slid her arms around his neck, rose on her knees so they were torso to torso.

He moaned, a mixture of need and frustration, then kissed her back—a raw, furious assault on her lips that had her head spinning and her blood racing.

Just as suddenly, he jerked away, his breathing ragged, his fingers biting painfully into her shoulders. His eyes were shadowed, fierce and violent.

But she wasn't afraid, she was exhilarated. She felt a sense of power she'd never experienced before, an inner strength she'd had no idea she possessed.

"I don't want your gratitude," he said between clenched teeth. "I don't want anything to happen here because of some misguided obligation or appreciation."

She smiled, touched her mouth to his and brushed her lips over his. Her own sense of calm amazed her. "This isn't about gratitude, Sam. This is about you and me. About what we're feeling, what we've both felt since the beginning."

She dropped kisses over his jaw, then down his neck. His body was like sculpted stone, the muscles of his shoulders and chest tightly bunched with restraint.

"Faith—" he swore as her hands moved restlessly over his arms and chest, then lower "—I want you. So bad it's killing me. But...I don't want to take advantage of you."

She laughed now. "I'm hardly the one being taken advantage of here, Sam." Her fingers dropped to the snap on his jeans.

Choking, he snatched hold of her wrists. "I want you to be sure."

"Is this sure enough?" She rubbed her cheek over his chest, pressed kisses to his heated skin. "Or this?" She shrugged the blanket off her shoulders, then arched her body into his, moving against him in a slow, sensuous rhythm that brought a curse to his lips.

He moved with lightning speed, caught her up in his arms so tightly she couldn't breathe. His mouth swooped down on hers, crushed her lips under his. For the second time that day, she felt helpless, carried on a raging, wild current. But this time she welcomed it, reveled in it, and the thought of drowning in pleasure this intense...this consuming...thrilled her.

Nothing had ever felt so right, so completely natural to her. A sense of belonging overwhelmed her. Here, in these mountains, in Sam's arms, with a glittering, star-filled ceiling and a bed of soft grass. Boston and all that waited for her there might as well have been a million miles away. For this moment, those things no longer existed. There was only her—and Sam.

She wrapped her arms around his neck, rose up to deepen his kiss. He tasted exciting, uncontrolled. Forbidden. The thought made her feel giddy, lightheaded, as did the kisses he now rained over her neck. She let her head slide back, exposing herself, her vulnerability, capitulating as a wild animal might yield to the more powerful foe.

"Make love to me, Sam," she whispered into his thick, dark hair. His lips nipped at the base of her throat, his evening beard scraping over her skin, sending sparks of electric heat skittering through her.

"I am, sweetheart. I am."

He devoured her with his mouth, his tongue, his hands—and she melted into him with a whimper. His hands skated down her back, slid over her rear; then upward to her breasts, cupping her fullness in his palms. Blood pounded through her chest, through her head, loud and pulsing. The rhythm of life, of love, of pleasure. It couldn't get any better than this, couldn't possibly feel any better, she thought dimly. She'd die if it did.

And when his mouth replaced his hands on her breasts she thought she just might die.

She gasped at the first pull of his teeth through the lace of her damp bra. From the deepest core of her body, a knot of intense pleasure braided and unbraided. His fingers slipped the straps from her shoulders, then slowly, maddeningly, traced the lacy edge down to the front clasp.

Wet lace fell away, only to be replaced by his hot

mouth. She clung to him, wrapped her hands around his arms to steady herself, bit her bottom lip to keep from crying out. But when he took her into his mouth, lavished the sensitive peak of her tightened nipple with his tongue and teeth, she did cry out. He made a low animal sound in response.

"Sam...." His name was a plea on her lips. Desire raged through her and still it wasn't enough. She wanted more, she wanted everything. From him, only from him.

He moved to her other breast, bestowed the same pleasure, his mouth and hands like liquid heat as they moved over her soft flesh. Like a bow, she arched her back, wantonly pressing herself closer. He accommodated her, taking her into his mouth, devouring her with his teeth and lips. She shuddered at the sensations ripping through her, felt dizzy and weak.

He thought he might never get enough of her. The curve of her slim hips; the flat, smooth line of her belly; the baby-soft swell of her breasts. He could taste the passion on her silky skin, hear the small sounds of need pulsing deep in her throat, feel the eager pull of her hands on his arms. He wanted to touch her everywhere at once, feel her skin on his.

He rose over her, dragging her body against his, smothering her lips with his. Her arms wrapped around his neck and she moved against him, slid her breasts over his bare chest, again and again, driving him out of his mind.

Her hands moved over his shoulders and arms, his chest, then downward, releasing the snap of his jeans. Her knuckles grazed the hard swell of his body as she slowly pulled the zipper down. He let out a slow breath.

Inch by inch, she tugged his wet jeans over his hips, not an easy feat, but she persevered until denim bunched around his knees. He kicked them off the rest of the way, then lowered her onto the blanket.

His eyes feasted.

The firelight danced on her pale naked body, illuminated her narrow waist and full breasts. Her eyes glowed with desire for him. No woman had ever made him feel this way, so powerful, so invincible. So out of control. Stunned at the realization, overwhelmed, he simply stared at her.

"You're beautiful." His voice was hoarse, his breathing rough.

The color on her cheeks rose, and her gaze slid away. He lay beside her, resting on his elbow as he leaned over her.

"Hey, I'm your husband, remember?" He cupped her chin in his palm and turned her face to his. He kissed her with featherlightness, then traced her swollen lips with his tongue. "I don't want you to be embarrassed with me, Faith."

She shook her head. "No one's ever looked at me like that before, ever said that to me."

Her confession shocked, but at the same time confused him. How was that possible? What man wouldn't see her breathtaking beauty, wouldn't tell her?

But this was no time to discuss past loves or experiences, for either one of them. Right now, all that mattered was that she was here, with him. He deepened the kiss, and she opened to him, flowed into his arms like melted honey.

"You're beautiful, too," she said shyly and fanned her hands over his chest.

Was there no end to the surprises from this woman? She was prim and proper one minute, a vamp the next, then suddenly shy and demure. Each woman excited him, intrigued him. Bewitched him.

He lowered his head, needing to explore the smooth column of her neck, the curve of her earlobe, the pulse beating rapidly at the base of her throat. He tangled his hands in her hair, tugged her head back, then came down on her mouth again, hungry for her, certain he could never get enough.

She writhed under him, thrust her hips toward his, driving him over the edge of sanity. He felt, more than heard, the groan deep in his throat. An urgency gripped him, clawed at his gut, and he jerked himself upright and knelt between her thighs. Her breasts thrust upward, an offering he found impossible to resist. He bent over her, cupped both in his palms, stroked each pearled nipple with the pads of his thumbs.

She moaned softly, and her fingers curled into the blanket underneath her.

"Open your eyes," he rasped.

She did as he asked, her heavy lids slowly opening, her eyes, dark blue, glazed with desire. He kissed the rosy tip of each breast, branded them with his tongue and his teeth. She arched upward.

"Keep them open," he commanded. "I want to watch you. I want to see your eyes when I'm inside you."

"Hurry," she whispered. "Please."

He hooked his thumbs in the lacy strip covering her hips—the last barrier between them—and slid them down, over her thighs, past her long, slender legs.

Exquisite, he thought, gazing down at her. Her body glistened in the firelight, her breasts still moist from his kisses. Never had he wanted so badly, so desperately. Her heated, smoky gaze met his, and she lifted her hips, opening to him, welcoming him.

The primitive urge to mate overpowered him, blinded him. In one swift, hard stroke, he drove himself into her.

Intense pleasure turned to shock.

A virgin.

Good Lord. Faith was a virgin.

With a willpower he didn't know he possessed, he went still. "Faith," he choked out, "sweetheart, you didn't, I mean, I didn't... My God..."

"Shh." She smiled, placed her hands on each side of his head. "It doesn't hurt, Sam. It's wonderful. You're wonderful."

"But—"

"I want you," she murmured. "I need you. Don't you know that? Can't you tell?"

He could, dammit. Her body hummed under his, begged for release, just as his body did. But that didn't change what he'd just done, what had just happened.

She arched upward, wrapped her legs around his. "Don't stop," she begged breathlessly. "Please don't stop."

Her plea broke the chain restraining him. Every

thought, every bit of reason splintered as she moved into him. He plunged deeply into her, the need consuming him—burning inside him, hotter and then hotter still. He caught her hips as she writhed under him and he moved into her, again and again, the fury building to fever pitch.

She cried out, burying her fingernails in his back, shuddering under him, through him, driving him to his own shattering release.

He collapsed, felt his senses slowly return while he dragged his mouth over hers, then gathered her to him and held her close in his arms.

"Why didn't you tell me?"

They were snuggled by the crackling fire, wrapped in the blanket and each other's arms. Shadows deepened and flickered, the scent of wild mint carried on the evening air. There was no perception of time for Faith. Of place, even. Just the incredible, wonderful feel of Sam's body against her own.

His quiet question held no accusation, she knew. They were beyond that. Way beyond.

"And if I had told you?" She traced the line of his strong jaw with her fingertip. "Would you have made love to me?"

"No. Yes. Hell, I don't know." He closed his eyes and sighed. "Yeah, I probably would have."

She stretched her body, pressing it more firmly to his. His sharp inhale of breath brought a smile to her face. She had never felt such a sense of satisfaction and contentment.

"Stop that." He tightened his hold on her to keep her still, but it only succeeded in bringing their bodies more intimately together. He groaned, then inched away. "Faith, we should have at least talked about it."

"I didn't feel like talking." A wanton woman had taken possession of her body, Faith decided, as she caressed his strong biceps. She decided she liked this woman.

"If you're expecting tears and recriminations, Sam, there won't be any. I'm not sorry. I knew what I was doing and I wouldn't change a thing." Her hand stopped suddenly and she frowned. "Are you sorry? Did I do something wrong?"

He swore, and without warning, rolled her onto her back. His gaze burned into hers. "Sorry? Hell, no. Did you do something wrong? Sweetheart, if you'd done anything *more* right, I swear I'd be dead right now."

Smiling, she breathed a sigh of relief, then touched his cheek. "So it wasn't just me, was it? It *was* incredible, wasn't it?"

"You're amazing." He took her hand in his, then pressed it lightly to his lips. "I just don't understand how it is, I mean— Damn, but this is awkward."

"How it is that I've never been with a man before?" she finished quietly. She'd never discussed her sex life—or lack of it—with anyone. Not even her mother. She knew that everyone assumed, because she and Harold were going to be married, that they were sleeping together. The fact was, she'd never been much interested, and had simply held him off with a number of excuses, promising that once they were married it would be so much more special. Being the patient, proper—understanding—man that he was, he'd never pushed.

Bold with her newfound power, she slid her hands again over his torso, surprised and delighted when his eyes darkened and narrowed in response. "My life has always been structured, planned to the minute. Part of that plan was to wait until I was married. I guess I'll have to make some adjustments in that department."

"You are married." The firelight glowed in his eyes. "To me. Remember?"

"I mean a real marriage, Sam. Mortgage, dog, children. The works."

"You make it sound like ordering a pizza." He skimmed her collarbone with his knuckles, held her gaze as he moved lower to the swell of her breast. Her breath quickened. "And not to throw another kink in your plans, but have you considered we didn't use any protection?"

She knew that both of their blood tests for the marriage licence had come back clean, so obviously he was implying that she might get pregnant.

A baby. She remembered holding little Madeline, Jake and Savannah's toddler. She'd felt something, something she'd never experienced before. A sense of wonder and affection. Her insides warmed just thinking about how they'd played—the honking and giggling. The little girl had felt so soft, smelled so nice. At least until she'd thrown up!

Faith had always known she'd have children, but she'd never once considered actually being a mother.

Certain it wasn't disappointment she felt, Faith met

Sam's studied gaze and slowly shook her head. "I'm on the pill."

Confusion furrowed his brow. "But...if you don't, if you haven't...."

She sat, turning her back to him, folding her arms to cover her nakedness. He had a right to ask, she supposed. She just suddenly felt so uncomfortable. They were two adults, for heaven's sake. *Intimate* adults. Why should she feel uneasy having a reasonable, logical discussion with him?

Because she was talking about another man. Her *fiancé*. The man she was supposed to—she was *going* to—marry.

Dammit. Why did her clothes have to be so far away?

"Sam, I'm...getting married, for real, in a few months. I needed to be...prepared. Harold and I were going to wait two or three years, until we're settled, and I have a few projects under control at Elijah Jane."

"Control." He ran a finger over her bare shoulders. "That's always the key word with you, isn't it, Faith?"

Even now, having this conversation, and as awkward as it was, she couldn't stop the shiver that coursed through her at his touch. She resisted the urge to lean back against him, to feel his skin against hers again. "I've told you I like to know where I'm going, what I'm doing. If it hadn't been for Digger throwing a wrench in my plans, I'd be in Boston right now."

"And this—" he said as his finger slid down her back "—this wasn't in your plans, either, was it?"

The rough texture of his finger on the sensitive skin

of her back started an ache throbbing within her. Need pumped through her body. How could it be there again so soon? And so strong? She closed her eyes, drew in a slow, deep breath. ''I don't regret making love with you, Sam.''

His hand paused. ''But?''

''But we're still two different people who live in two different worlds. That hasn't changed.''

His finger slipped away from her. She felt cold. Confused. And so incredibly alone.

He stood, walked to his backpack and pulled out a pair of dry jeans. She glanced at him, felt her heart beat faster. His body was carved of solid muscle, his shoulders broad, his waist narrow. When he bent over to tug on the jeans, those muscles rippled and danced.

Only minutes before, she'd slid her hands over that magnificent body, experienced a passion she'd never dreamed existed. The realization that she wanted to experience it again, with him, brought heat to her cheeks. She looked quickly away, then tugged the blanket over her shoulders.

She heard the hiss of his zipper, the snap of his jeans. ''I'll get your clothes.''

''Thank you.''

So polite. So stiff. She watched him walk toward the hot springs and closed her eyes on a long sigh.

She'd lied when she'd said she didn't regret making love with him. She did regret it. Because now that she had...now that she knew...her life was never going to be the same.

Eight

He didn't wake up in a good mood. But then he hadn't exactly gone to sleep in a good mood, either. He'd closed his eyes, several times in fact, but he couldn't quite remember if he'd ever actually gone to sleep.

How the hell was he supposed to sleep with Faith lying two feet away?

He snapped the blanket onto his horse's back, drawing an annoyed, sidelong glance from the gelding. He knew he shouldn't take out his bad mood on his horse; it wasn't the animal's fault that his owner was irritable as a grizzly. It had much more to do with a slender blonde from Boston with baby-blue eyes. Eyes that made him feel as if he were drowning.

He couldn't count the times he'd nearly gone to her during the night, the times he'd had to stop himself from dragging her into his sleeping bag with him. He cursed himself for making love with her, then cursed himself again because he ached to make love with her again.

He could have gone to her; he was confident she would have welcomed him, though she certainly hadn't said so with words. They'd barely spoken at all after they'd dressed. But he'd seen it in her eyes. At dinner, as they'd cleaned up afterward, when they'd laid out their sleeping bags. The need had been there, the longing. He not only recognized it, he'd felt it himself to the point of pain.

He wanted her. She wanted him. Why should that be complicated?

It had never been complicated before. His relationships with women had always been easy. He enjoyed women. Loved the way they smelled, the way they walked, the way their bodies curved. He'd sparred with several, but managed to dodge any direct hits.

But Faith Courtland had scored a knockout.

She'd devastated him. He'd wanted her from the first moment he'd seen her, but the want had been purely physical. This—whatever *this* was—was something entirely different.

He cinched the saddle and glanced over his shoulder at her. She sat on a rock by the small fire he'd built earlier, braiding her hair as she stared at the flames. Under her denim jacket she wore a white tank top, and with her arms lifted, her breasts pressed tightly against it. His throat went dry as desert sand.

Pride was a hell of a beast.

It was his own damn fault, he knew. He'd asked questions, she'd answered them. Honestly. He couldn't blame her because he hadn't liked what she'd told him.

From the beginning, he'd known that she was going to marry another man. Their own marriage was no more than a business deal, a temporary convenience to satisfy Digger's will. She would have her presidency of Elijah Jane. He'd have another twenty-thousand acres. Simple.

Only it wasn't simple. Not anymore. He could tell himself he felt that way because of last night, because he felt a sense of responsibility, because he was the first man she'd ever been with. But he knew it went further than that, much further. And if he was going to be honest, dammit, then the fact was, he was glad he was the first. Somehow, it didn't matter that this was the nineties. He felt something very primitive—possessive even—about knowing that she'd been his alone.

And realizing all that made him mad as hell. So did all that talk about that idiot she was going to marry. How could she marry that jerk? She wasn't in love with him. It was so damn obvious.

He turned to look at her again. She'd finished braiding her hair and was kicking sand on the fire to close up camp. Damn, but she was beautiful. The mountains agreed with her. Her cheeks had a rosy glow, her eyes were bright and alert, her shoulders relaxed.

No, she wasn't in love with that other guy, he thought firmly, slapping a saddle on his horse. She couldn't be.

And before this trip was through, before they were through, she was going to realize it.

* * *

"Are we almost there?"

She felt like a child, asking Sam for the tenth time when they were going to reach Digger's camp. Of course, if he'd given her something specific, instead of one of his vague answers, she wouldn't have to keep asking. Twice, he'd simply grunted at her.

He glanced over his shoulder. "Not long."

Two whole words. Wow. He must be loosening up.

With a heavy sigh, she settled back in her saddle. Why was he being so tight-lipped? Was he upset with her because of last night? Because she hadn't told him that she was a virgin? Was it regret that furrowed his brow? Or was it all that talk about Harold?

Tears burned in her eyes, but she blinked them away. Her chest ached, but she ignored it. She refused to let his surly attitude destroy her memory of the most wonderful experience of her life.

He'd risked his life for her, made love to her, given her something more incredible than she could ever have imagined—and now he wouldn't even speak to her.

She'd never understand the man.

Her fingers tightened on her reins. It was too beautiful a day to be upset. The sky was deep blue, with wisps of white cotton-candy clouds. Bees hummed, purple martins gurgled, a breeze cooled the sun-warm air. So maybe he had thrown her off balance, unsettled her. She'd bounce back. She'd spent a lifetime bouncing back.

Once they finished their business here in the mountains and were back at the ranch, it would be easier to avoid Sam—to keep her distance. The remainder of the two months would fly by. She'd be back in

Boston and married. President of Elijah Jane. She'd have everything she'd ever wanted.

Wouldn't she?

"Here we are."

Startled from her musing, Faith realized that they'd entered a large, flat cove, with the mountains on one side and the river on the other. Cut into the mountain, crude steps led up about twenty feet to what appeared to be a cave. A mine, she realized.

Her heart slammed in her chest.

This was it. Where Digger left the rest of the world behind. He'd worked here, alone, unrelenting, searching for his dream.

Her knees felt weak as she dismounted. Though the current in the river was swift here, it wasn't as fast as it had been near the hot springs, nor as deep. It seemed so peaceful here. Calm.

It was hard to believe a man had died here.

Not just any man. Her father.

"You okay?"

She hadn't realized that Sam had walked up behind her. She turned to face him, shoving her hands into her front pockets so he wouldn't see them shaking. "Fine. Is this the place... Is this where it happened?"

He nodded slowly. "He always made camp right here, on the river. He had a tent set up maybe fifteen feet away from the edge."

She looked to the shore of the river, but saw nothing.

"It's gone," he said quietly. "The flood hit fast and hard, washed everything away. The only thing we found was one of his boots, about half a mile from here."

The image formed ice in her veins. She remembered her own close call yesterday, how easily a strong current could carry a person away. How quickly. A flood like the one Sam described would have been ten times worse. "How do you know the boot was his?"

"Digger was the only person who ever came down into here. It was his size, exactly the kind of boot he wore." His voice became gentle. "There was no doubt, Faith."

"But his horse..." she insisted. "How could an animal that size just disappear?"

"Just like a man. Washed away, sometimes miles. Under dirt and branches and rocks."

She no longer heard the birds chirping or the sound of bees. The sun that had felt so warm only a short while ago was dipping low in the sky, and the evening air had taken on a chill. "I'd like to look around for a while. Before it gets too dark."

"I'll settle the animals in and set up camp." He took her reins. "There're still a few things of his up in the mine if you want to go inside. The lantern should have some fuel, and matches are on the bench."

Heart pounding, knees trembling, she took the steps slowly, carefully. The opening of the mine swelled before her; its dark, silent mouth drew her in. She stepped inside, let her eyes adjust to the dim light, then moved to a small bench against one wall of the mine and lit the lantern.

Rock walls glowed. The air was cooler inside, damp and musty; the dirt under her feet, soft. She drew in a slow, deep breath.

There were picks and hammers on the bench, a stack of moldy paperback books, and a coffee can filled with chunks of rock and dirt. She picked up a handful of small stones, let them sift through her fingers back into the can, then picked up the lantern and walked into the darkness.

The can of spaghetti and meatballs he'd opened was warming over the fire. The pasta would be mushy, the meatballs would be like cardboard, but after a long day of riding he knew it would taste as good as any gourmet meal. He'd shared more than a few cans with Digger. Right on this very spot. They'd mined, fished, camped out together for more than twenty years. He thought that he'd known Digger Jones better than anyone.

But he hadn't. He'd never really known him at all. No one had.

Least of all, Faith.

He glanced up at the mine opening. She'd been up there a long time. Too long, he thought, considering there wasn't much to see. A few dusty tools, a couple of cooking pots, some reading material. Two months ago, out of respect for Digger, everything had been left as they'd found it. The mine shaft, a five-foot wide, forty-foot deep tunnel, had been boarded up, just in case someone happened along and decided to explore. But the cave itself, where it was flat, cut into the mountain no more than twenty feet.

So what the hell was taking her so long?

Uneasy, he rose from the rock he'd been sitting on and stared into the darkness. He'd told her that they'd already thoroughly searched the mine shaft two months ago, before they closed it up. There had been no body in there, no doubt about it.

But then, he'd also told her that they'd never found a body *anywhere,* and she'd still insisted she wanted to see for herself. Why would this time be any different?

He frowned. She wouldn't be that foolish. Especially after she'd nearly drowned yesterday. The woman couldn't possibly be that careless or thoughtless of danger.

Still, a knot of fear began to tighten in his stomach. He'd never seen a woman more determined, more tenacious. More stubborn. The mine shaft might tempt her; she might try for just one look.

And fall forty feet into a dark, cold hole.

He swung around, already taking a step toward the mine, when he stopped. She stood on the edge of the darkness, between the firelight and the shadows.

He waited, letting his pulse slow down and his fear drain away. She moved closer, stopped beside the fire, but said nothing. She had a paperback book tucked under one arm and an old coffee can clutched against her stomach.

''Spaghetti and meatballs.'' Her expression was blank, her eyes empty and tired. ''Did I ever tell you that Elijah Jane is thinking about starting a line of canned goods? We thought we'd start with chili.''

''Why don't you sit down,'' he said gently. ''I'll get you something to eat.''

''If it goes well, we'll add a soup line, too.''

She looked so pale beside the fire, so lost. Her eyes met his, but he knew he might as well be a ghost right now.

"Faith, please." He felt helpless, completely powerless to stop whatever it was going on inside her. "Come sit."

"I'm trying to imagine what it was like." Unblinking, she stared at the flames. "To hole yourself away, alone in a dark world, chipping away at rock, hour after hour, day after day."

He realized that she wasn't talking to him, so he kept quiet. But he'd never seen her like this—so distant, so detached. He struggled to keep from reaching for her.

She held up the coffee can. "And at the end of your life all you'd have left to show for all that backbreaking, lonely work was a rusty can of pebbles?"

She reached into the can, closed her fingers tightly around a rock, then tossed it into the fire.

"He had a picture of me. My high school graduation." She pulled a photograph from the paperback, then dropped the book on the ground. "I found it between page two hundred thirty-six and two hundred thirty-seven of Mark Twain's *Life on the Mississippi.* He read the classics. Hemingway, Fitzgerald, Steinbeck. Another surprise."

He *was* surprised. He hadn't looked at the titles when he'd been in the mine before. She'd not only looked at them, she'd picked them up, leafed through them. And found a picture of herself. "Faith, just let me—"

He moved toward her, but she shied away. Her eyes were alert now, bright with anger. "I had a right to know. They owed me that much."

"No one wanted to hurt you. Digger, your mother, Joseph. They all loved you."

"Oh, yes, Joseph. Aren't I the lucky one." Her voice was brittle. "I had two fathers. One I could never please, who was rarely home...and one who wanted nothing to do with me."

She stared at the photograph. "You want to hear something funny, something I've never told anyone? When I was little I used to fantasize about having another father. A real father who would come and take me and my mother and we'd go live somewhere, maybe even on a mountain. That's what foolish dreams get you, Sam. Disappointment and a can full of worthless rocks."

She threw the can into the fire, spilling rocks into the crackling flames. Sparks flew from the sudden assault.

"Damn you, Digger Jones." She crumpled the photograph in her hand. "Damn you to hell."

The picture sailed through the air, into the fire. It burst into flame, hissed, then melted into black ash. Wide-eyed, she stared at the fire, then covered her mouth with her hands.

"Oh, my God." Despair darkened her eyes. "What have I done?"

He took hold of her shaking shoulders, pulled her rigid body against him. "It's just a picture, sweetheart. It doesn't matter."

"That's what I told myself. When I found out that Digger was my father...when I went to his funeral. Even when we got married. I told myself it didn't matter, that as long as I held onto control of Elijah Jane, everything else was unimportant."

Her fingers gripped his shirt, and she looked up at

him. He saw the anguish there, but there was nothing he could do but hold her.

"I was wrong, Sam. About everything. I might have told myself it didn't matter, but this time I was the one lying to myself. It did matter. I didn't want him to be dead. I wanted to tell him to his face that I hated him, that he'd let me down, that my mother had been miserable. If he wasn't alive, I had to see it for myself, to be sure, so I could let go of it all and get on with my life…be free of the anger."

Though she resisted, he pulled her close, gently and persistently. Even after she'd fallen in the river yesterday and faced death, she hadn't been this vulnerable, this fragile. She'd pulled herself together, dealt with it and moved on. But now this, facing—and accepting—the death of her father, this was her undoing.

"But I don't hate him," she said quietly. "I want to, but I don't. I just hate that I was lied to. That I never had a chance to know him."

Shuddering, she sagged against him. "You must think I'm such a wimp."

He laughed softly and kissed the top of her head. "Darlin', of all the things I think of you, wimp doesn't even come close."

She sniffed. "That was another lie I told myself. That what you thought about me didn't matter. It does matter." Her hands slid up to his neck, then cupped his face as she eased back and looked up at him. "Very much."

He kissed her, a light brush of his lips over hers. "I think you are the most amazing, incredible, sexy, intelligent, dazzling woman I've ever met."

She smiled against his lips, bestowing feather-soft kisses. ''I like sexy and dazzling,'' she murmured. ''Don't stop now.''

Chuckling, he kissed her cheek, then her jaw. ''Beautiful, astonishing, extraordinary.'' He moved to the base of her throat, then skimmed his lips over her neck, her shoulder.

''That's not what I meant, Sam.'' She buried her fingers in his hair and dragged his mouth back to hers. ''This is what I meant.''

The frustration, the need that had been building inside him all day shattered with her breathless words. He crushed his mouth against hers with an urgency he'd never known before, deepening the kiss, slanting his mouth hard against hers again and again. She moaned in response, molding her lips and her body to his. Blood pounded in his temples, heat poured through his veins.

How could he ever have thought he'd be able to keep his distance from this woman? He could do that no more than he could stop the river from flowing or the sun from rising. He needed her as desperately as he needed his next breath. She was everything he'd told her and more, so much more. And for this moment, if only for this moment, she was his.

''I want your legs around me,'' he said roughly, cupping her bottom in his large hands. ''I need to feel you against me.''

He lifted her, and she wrapped her long, lean legs around his waist. She arched into him, pressing her breasts against his chest, then made room for her hands to slide between their bodies. Impatient, she tugged at the buttons on his shirt, then shoved the fabric aside. The touch of her smooth, soft fingers over his bare skin sent spears of white-hot pleasure through him, and he closed his eyes on a moan. Her mouth never left his, and she matched his kisses with an eager insistence that set his blood on fire.

Tightening his hold on her, he moved to the sleeping bags already laid out by the fire. Though only a few feet away, for Faith it felt like miles—an endless journey. This was what she wanted, what she desperately needed. For the first time in her life she understood what it really felt like to be a woman in every way. She'd needed to lose that part of her so that she might feel whole, and the power of this newfound freedom overwhelmed her. If only she had the words, she would tell him what he'd given her, how much he meant to her.

And even if she could find the words, what he was doing to her with his hands and his mouth, the way he made her head spin and her body tremble, rendered her speechless. She could only feel, and the sensations were so intense, so glorious, she thought she might come apart in his arms.

Her heart leaped as he lowered her, slowly sliding her body down his, maximizing contact. She burned every agonizing inch of the way, torn between wishing that this sweet agony could last forever and praying that he would hurry.

He was in no hurry.

With his arms wrapped tightly around her, her feet barely touched the ground. His mouth caught hers again, his assault ruthless, relentless. She tangled her fingers in his hair and opened to him, greedy for more. He accommodated her, his tongue finding hers, the rhythm as primitive as it was savage, as driving as it was insistent. Dizzy with desire, she met him stroke for stroke, moaned with the pleasure streaking through her veins.

Slowly he lowered her onto the sleeping bags. The ground was soft against her back, a cushion of thick down and plush earth. The scent of sage hung heavy in the night air; the moon, full and bright, bathed the canyon in a silver glow and danced off the raging river. Everything felt like a dream—a wonderful, incredible fantasy come to life. Wrapping her arms around Sam's neck, she pulled him down to her, knowing that she could never want again as she wanted now, could never need any man as much as she needed this one.

The thought made her hesitate, frightened her even, but then, with his mouth trailing hot kisses down her neck, she couldn't think at all.

She felt...as no man had ever made her feel before, and no man, she was certain, would ever make her feel again. He cupped her breasts, kneading her soft flesh until she heard herself whimper. His lips moved lower; buttons tumbled free of their enclosures; the front clasp of her bra snapped open; the cool air skimmed her bared breasts. Then his head lowered and he took her hardened, aching nipple into his mouth.

A muffled, primal scream rumbled deep in her throat. She strained upward and hungrily he took what she offered. His tongue, hot and moist, stroked; his teeth nipped and tugged. Golden arrows of intense pleasure shot straight through her, to her very center.

"Sam, please. Now," she gasped.

But still he took his time. While his mouth and lips lavished attention on one breast, he palmed the other, brushing the sensitive nipple with the pad of his thumb. He molded and kneaded, turning her inside out, driving her crazy with his sensual feast of her body.

But it wasn't enough. She wanted more; she needed all. All of him. Not just the physical, but more, much more.

She shivered as he moved over her, brought her to life, made her feel with an intensity she would never have believed she possessed. And though she knew there was no place to take this, the only thing that mattered at this moment was being with him. She wanted to remember everything, every sound, every brush of his lips, every soft murmur. She would carry this with her forever. In her thoughts, in her heart.

Curling her fingers into the fabric of his shirt, she forced him onto his back. She straddled him as she tugged his shirt from his jeans and shoved it upward, baring his broad chest. She dragged her hands downward, raking her nails over his skin, through the mat of coarse hair, over his flat, muscled stomach. She followed the V lower still until her fingers slid over his belt buckle; then lower still, over the hard masculine bulge beneath his zipper. She heard the sharp intake of his breath, felt him move beneath her hands, and gloried in the realization that he wanted her as badly as she wanted him.

The belt buckle fell away under her fingers; the snap of his jeans came open; the zipper hissed apart. His belly was smooth under her hands, his skin hot. When she slipped her fingertips under the band of his briefs he jolted upright, catching her wrists and dragging her up against him. Bare skin met bare skin. She wrapped her arms and legs around him and rubbed her breasts against his chest. Pleasure streaked through her at the erotic contact.

He groaned, a low, deep animal sound, crushing his mouth against hers, kissing her deeply.

And then she was on her back, staring up into eyes as dark as the night, like black ice, intense, with a hint of danger. He tugged at her boots and jeans. Gasping, she helped him with his. He moved over her, slid between her legs and drew them tightly around him. With his eyes still holding hers, he locked his hands with hers and raised them over her head. When he buried himself deep inside her, she cried out, arching upward to meet him.

He began to move, a rhythm that had her biting her bottom lip, nearly crying with the pleasure consuming her. Though it hardly seemed possible, he grew larger inside her, harder. He thrust again and again, faster, higher. She writhed under him, her hands clasped in his, calling his name over and over, a wild desperate plea. He answered her, his words erotic, seductive, carnal. Words that should have shocked her, but instead, excited and aroused.

Straining, breathless, she met him thrust for thrust, drew him deeper still into her body until she thought she might go mad with the tension inside her. The feelings were too intense, too strong…and a scream began to build deep within her.

"Sam!"

The scream burst from her as pleasure exploded through her body. She shuddered from the incredible force of it, felt Sam's body tighten, then heard the deep guttural moan of his own release.

Breath ragged, his heart beating furiously, he collapsed on her.

Smiling, she pulled her arms free and wrapped them around his sweat-dampened shoulders.

He kissed her long and hard, then lifted his head. "I'm too heavy."

"No." She held him in place when he started to rise. "I want you right here."

He grinned at her, shifted his hips. "Right *here,* huh?"

She sucked in a breath.

"Or maybe right here?" He kissed her neck, shifted his hips again slightly.

She moaned softly.

His lips trailed over her neck, down to her breast. "Tell me what you want, sweetheart," he murmured, moving inside her with determined precision.

"I want you, Sam," she whispered and brought his mouth back to hers. "Only you."

He pulled away, stared down at her, said nothing—but the intensity in his eyes burned into her. Then he kissed her, slowly, deeply, tenderly. He made her tremble, made her want, made her need.

Pulling him to her, she surrendered to the bliss of his touch and lost herself to him once again.

The sun rose much too early the next morning. But then, after a night of lovemaking with Sam, Faith was certain that noon would have been too early.

Cracking one eye open, she realized that she was alone in the sleeping bag. The heat of his body still lingered beside her and she rolled into the warmth of it, running her hand over the soft flannel lining as she recalled the hours she'd just spent in his arms.

The man was insatiable.

Perhaps she'd been a little greedy herself, she thought, smiling, and pulled on the sweatshirt and sweatpants from the backpack beside her.

Her smile widened. Okay, she admitted, and snuggled back down inside the sleeping bag. A lot greedy.

"Rise and shine, Sleeping Beauty."

He stood over her, a towel draped over one shoulder and water dripping from the ends of his slicked-back hair. She thought it unfair he looked so damn handsome this early in the morning, especially after so little sleep. She knew she must look awful, with her hair a mess and her eyes sleepy.

He knelt beside her, and when she started to hide under the covers, took her chin in his hand. He kissed her lightly, then smiled. "Damn, but I can't wait to get you into a bed."

She laughed and rolled out of the sleeping bag. He started to grab for her, but she ducked under his arm, giggling as he tackled her and pushed her onto her back. He leaned over her, holding her hands at her sides as he bent to kiss her again. She waited, breath held, pulse racing, for his lips to meet hers.

"Hallo!"

Faith's eyes flew open at the deep, gravelly voice of an intruder. Sam stiffened, then slowly turned.

"Who is it?" she whispered frantically. She sat, then craned her neck to see around Sam's shoulders.

A man leading a black mare emerged from a group of cottonwoods by the river. A tall man. With silver hair and beard.

Digger.

Nine

It wasn't possible. He had to be dreaming. Sam blinked, certain when he looked again at the man walking toward them that it would be someone else—someone who just looked like Digger, sounded like Digger.

With the same lumbering swagger, the same small-brimmed straw hat.

The man waved and called out again.

Sam's heart stopped, then raced.

My God. It *was* Digger.

Or else it was a ghost. A ghost who looked and sounded not only alive, but healthy, as well. With a thin cigar clamped between his teeth, at that.

"Well, now, if it isn't Sammy." Digger stopped several feet away and tipped his hat back. "What brings you up here, son?"

"Digger?" Sam's voice was a whisper.

Faith's fingers tightened on his arm. He heard her breath catch, but still, he couldn't take his eyes off Digger. For that matter, he couldn't move at all.

"Well, it ain't Grizzly Adams, boy, though I admit, I am looking a little ragged at the moment."

He was. His beard was longer, his hair pulled back into a ponytail. "But you....Good God, man, we thought you were dead."

"Dead!" His guffaw echoed through the trees. "Why in the hell would you think that?"

Very slowly, through the haze of confusion blanketing his brain, Sam searched for words. "We... came looking for you after the flood. Your camp was gone...you were gone. And when you didn't show up after you'd told Matilda you'd only be gone two weeks, we all assumed you'd drowned."

"Two weeks! I told Matilda I'd be gone two months. And I wasn't at my camp. I've been working a new mine couple miles south of here. Didn't even know there was a flood through here till now." He frowned at the spot where his tent had been, then shook his head. "Damn. Looks like I'm gonna have to git me a new rig here."

Still in shock, Sam could only stare. "Digger, we had a funeral for you."

He raised his brows. "You don't say?"

"Dammit, man, we thought you were dead!"

"Well, I'm not." Digger glanced behind Sam. "Why, Sammy, whatcha hiding there under that sleeping bag? A woman?"

Faith. Good Lord. What was this going to do to

her? How would she handle meeting Digger like this? "Digger, listen, there's something you should—"

"Don't be shy, boy." Digger tossed his reins over his horse's saddle and grinned. "Let's bring the filly out here and have a look-see."

"No. Wait—"

"I'm not a *filly,* Mr. Jones." Arms held tight by her sides, Faith stood and faced Digger. "I'm your daughter."

Digger's grin froze. He hesitated, then slowly took the cigar out of his mouth. "Well, I'll be damned."

She held her gaze level with his as she rose. "My thoughts exactly."

He nodded slowly. "Don't reckon I'd blame you none there."

They stood facing each other—father and daughter—neither one moving, both waiting.

Faith started to sway and Sam moved toward her, but she backed away, lifting her chin as she drew in a slow breath. "Sam, why don't you make some coffee and keep *my father* company while I go change? I'll just be a minute or two."

Sam stood slowly, amazed at Faith's ability to pull herself together so quickly, to calmly face Digger and offer coffee as if he'd been invited for cake and cookies.

But then he saw the quiver in her fingers as she reached for her backpack, the ashen tint to her skin. She wasn't calm. She was scared to death. This was her way to handle this, he realized, the only way she knew. She'd give herself a minute alone, pull herself together, then face the father she'd never known.

A man who had come back from the dead.

She stood and looked at Digger, her gaze steady and even, then turned smoothly, walked into the trees and disappeared behind an outcrop of boulders.

Sam turned back to Digger and saw him staring at the spot where Faith had been. A look he'd never seen before shone in the old man's blue eyes—a look of such longing—such love—that Sam felt as if he were intruding.

As if pulling himself out of a dream, Digger dragged his gaze back to Sam. "She's something, isn't she, Sammy?"

Sam couldn't help but smile. Who would ever have thought? Digger, the proud parent. "Yeah, Digger," he answered quietly. "That, she is."

Sam stared at his friend, took in his worn jeans, the patched woolen jacket and scuffed boots. He looked like something the proverbial cat had dragged in.

And he'd never looked better.

Shaking his head, Sam threw his arms around Digger. "Welcome back, you son of a bitch." They hugged and slapped each other on the back.

Then Digger nodded in the direction Faith had gone. "Did she tell you? About me and her mother?"

Sam nodded. "And about Elijah Jane Corporation, with a net worth of twenty-million dollars, owned by Francis Elijah Montgomery, more commonly known to the town of Cactus Flat as Digger Jones."

Shrugging, Digger jammed his cigar back in his mouth. "It was bound to come out sooner or later."

"Bound to come out sooner or later? Digger, for God's sake, why would you hide such a thing? You didn't have to lie to anyone. We're all your friends here.''

''Sammy—'' Digger said patiently ''—you know well as me that if folks found out I had that kind of money they'd treat me different. They wouldn't see plain old Digger Jones, they'd see dollar bills all over me. Besides, I never lied to no one. Just kept my business private. Man's got a right to that.''

It was true, of course, Sam knew. The town, his friends, they all would have looked at Digger differently.

''Okay, so you have a good point there.'' Sam rubbed a hand over his face. ''And a man does have a right to keep his own business private. But what he doesn't have the right to do is interfere in other people's business.''

Digger's eyes narrowed. ''I don't butt in where I'm not wanted.''

Sam gave a dry snort of laughter. ''What the hell do you call that interesting little condition in your will about Faith marrying me?''

Digger shifted his cigar from one side of his mouth to the other. ''Oh. Well, that was a proposition, that's all.''

''Proposition?'' Sam's single swear word was raw and to the point. ''It was nothing short of blackmail! You knew how badly Faith wanted the presidency of Elijah Jane, and how much I needed that land.''

''Blackmail's a hard word, Sammy. She had a choice, and so did you.'' He hesitated, then a slow grin spread over his face. ''So you did it, then? You two are hitched?''

''You play God with two people's lives and that's

all you can say? Did we get hitched?'' Sam put his hands on his hips and shook his head. ''You're unbelievable.''

''You did, didn't you?'' Digger tossed his cigar into the ashes of last night's fire and threw his arms around Sam. ''Hot damn!''

Sam's teeth vibrated from the force of Digger's hug. ''Dammit, Digger, stop that. This is serious.''

''Damn straight, it is.'' Digger gave Sam another bone-crunching squeeze, then released him. ''I knew it. I knew you two were right for each other.''

''Faith was—*is*—'' he had to bite down on the word ''—engaged to another man. She's getting married in a few months.''

''Well, now—'' Digger lifted one eyebrow ''—she can't very well marry someone else if she's married to you, can she?''

Something passed through Sam, as vague as it was elusive. ''Our marriage is temporary, Digger. Two months, if you remember. Then Faith is free to marry whomever she wants. And the man she wants is back in Boston. You must have known that.''

Digger waved a hand of dismissal. ''Her mother told me. Some uptight, stuffed shirt named Arnold.''

Sam shook his head. ''Howard,'' he corrected.

''Harold.''

Both men turned at the sound of Faith's voice. She stood at the edge of the trees, dressed in jeans and a dark blue cotton shirt, hair combed into a ponytail. Her eyes were as cool as her tone, her lips set in a thin line.

''His name is Harold,'' she said again, moving toward them, keeping her gaze on Digger. ''But you wouldn't know that, would you? In fact, you don't know anything about me, do you, *Dad?*"

"I'll just take a walk." Sam turned to leave.

"Stay right there, Sam. You've been dragged into this, and you deserve some answers, too."

Besides, Faith thought, the idea of being alone with Digger—with this father she'd never known—terrified her. Her heart was pounding so hard in her chest she felt certain that both men could hear it.

Digger Jones. Francis Elijah Montgomery. Her father. Standing three feet from her.

Alive.

She wanted to cry, she wanted to laugh, she wanted to scream. She did none of those things.

She faced him—this tall, bear of a man. There were deep lines on his face: lines of a lifetime, lines of hard work, lines of long days in the outdoors. His eyes were pale blue—the same color as hers, she realized with a jolt. She stared into those eyes, and saw a softness there that surprised her.

"I know you've been through a lot, honey," Digger said gently. "Why don't we all just sit down and talk awhile. Sort things out."

"Sort things out?" She repeated, feeling a bubble of hysteria in her throat. "You've lied to me... manipulated me...and you think we should just sit down calmly and *sort things out?*"

"I only want what's best for you, Faith. That's all I've ever wanted."

"I suppose that's why you left my mother, let her marry a man she didn't love." She saw the flash of pain in his eyes. "Because that was best for me."

He sighed, sat on a rock and rested his arms on his

knees. "I wanted to marry your mama, more than I'd ever wanted anything in my life. It cut likc a knife in my gut when I got that letter from your granddaddy. By the time I decided to face her, make her tell me to my face she didn't want me, she was already married to Joseph. As much as I loved her, I started thinking maybe your granddaddy was right. Maybe she *did* deserve better than me. And you, Faith. You deserved a father you could be proud of. Not an old miner like me."

"Do you think any of that mattered to my mother? She loved you," Faith said, her throat thick with tears. "Nobody thought enough of her to give her a choice."

He shook his head. "I thought the world of her. That's why I let her—why I let you—go. I'm a simple man, Faith. Back then, I was poor, too. No education. All I owned was a few rock picks and some recipes passed on from my grandpappy. But your mama—" he smiled then, a wry slow curve of the lips "—well, she was something else. The minute she walked into Leo's Sandwich Shop and ordered a turkey on wheat, she dazzled me, blinded me. With her soft blonde hair and sad green eyes, she was the prettiest thing I'd ever seen. You look just like her."

Embarrassed by Digger's compliment, yet strangely warmed, Faith glanced at Sam. He was leaning back against a sycamore, his arms folded, watching quietly. What would it be like to dazzle a man like that? To blind him, as Digger had said. To have him speak of you as if you were the most precious thing in the world?

An ache spread through her. If only things had been different…if her life had been different….

"Faith." Digger pulled her attention back to him. "What are you doing here, in Lonesome Rock Canyon?"

"They said you were dead," she said quietly. "I… needed to know, to be sure…."

He watched her for a long moment, then nodded slowly. "I'm sorry if I hurt you or your mama. That's the last thing I'd ever want to do."

Confused, her head still spinning, Faith looked back at Sam. He was a part of all this, whether he wanted it or not. She drew in a long, slow breath and faced Digger—her father—again.

"Why Sam?" she asked. "Why did you bring him into this…force him to marry me?"

"You don't know Sammy very well if you think anybody could force that boy into anything." Digger looked at Sam and grinned. "The land might have got him thinking, but it wouldn't have made up his mind. If he married you, he did it because he wanted to."

For an instant she thought maybe she saw something in Sam's eyes, something that might validate Digger's statement—that maybe, just possibly, he had married her for some reason other than the land.

No, she chided herself—that was wishful thinking. It wasn't possible, no matter what Digger said.

"I just wanted you to be happy, Faith. I thought maybe you and Sammy…." Digger sighed. "Well, maybe it was a bad idea, after all. For both of you."

She should be the first one to agree with him. Of

course it was a bad idea. It was on the tip of her tongue to tell him exactly that.

But, she thought, it hadn't been so bad. In fact, it hadn't been bad at all.

It had been wonderful.

The realization shocked her. She'd enjoyed being Mrs. Sam McCants, even if it hadn't been for real. She'd found something these past few days with Sam: a sense of herself, a happiness and contentment she'd never known before. She'd always be grateful to Sam for that.

She might feel anger toward Digger for a lot of things, but not for forcing her to marry Sam. For that, she was grateful.

But she certainly had no intention of telling him that. Especially at the moment, with Sam watching her so closely.

"How 'bout I ride back to Sammy's ranch with you?" He took off his hat, then settled it back on his head. "We get to know each other a little. See how it fits. Then whatever you decide 'bout you and me, I'll accept."

He made it sound so simple. So easy. Why didn't it feel that way? "And Elijah Jane?"

"No conditions. If you still want it, the presidency is yours."

President of Elijah Jane! Weren't those the words she'd wanted to hear? Why she'd come here? Why she'd married Sam, even? She should be elated, thrilled.

So why wasn't she?

She looked at Sam again. His mouth was set in a firm line, his eyes masked as he stared back at her.

With Digger alive, he had an out now. They both did. Based on fraud, their marriage could be annulled easily.

Did he want that?

Did she?

What a ridiculous thought. Of course he did...and she did, too. They each had their own life to live.

She turned back to Digger. "What about Sam's twenty-thousand acres?"

Digger grinned. "It's all his, honey. Every square inch. After all I put you two through, it's the least I can do."

After all he'd put them through. An image of herself in Sam's arms and him making love to her brought a flush to her cheeks. She glanced at Sam and saw the smile in his eyes.

"So how 'bout some breakfast?" He slapped his knees and stood. "I'll whip us up some buckwheat hotcakes with wild blueberries while you tell me all about my funeral. It's not every day a man gets to hear about his own final send-off."

He started for his horse, then stopped suddenly and looked at Sam. "Did that fool deputy come to the service?"

At Sam's nod, Digger grunted. "Damn hypocrite. I still ain't gonna let him eat at the diner. No one gives me a parking ticket and gets away with it."

Biting back a laugh, Faith looked at Sam. Shaking his head, Sam moved beside her and together they watched Digger unload his backpack. "Well, sweetheart, looks like you got what you came here for. You can go home a happy woman."

Go home a happy woman? There was no malice in

his voice, no sarcasm, and still his simple statement sliced through her like a knife.

"Hey!" Digger pulled out a frying pan. "I told Fitcher I wanted the deluxe package—oak casket and lots of roses. What'd I git?"

Sam shook his head at the absurdity of Digger's question. "You even got Madge on the organ, Digger. First class all the way. Church was packed, and we had a real nice party for you at the hotel, too."

Digger grinned, then grabbed a pail and headed for the river, whistling *Amazing Grace.*

Chuckling, Sam turned back to Faith. "Damned if I'm not glad he's alive."

She nodded. "Me, too."

He moved beside her and tucked a loose strand of hair behind her ear as he bent closer. "You know what else I'm glad about?" he whispered.

She shivered at the touch of his hand brushing her ear, at the husky sound of his voice. "What?"

"That in two days we'll be back at the ranch."

"Oh." Her heart sank. So he couldn't wait to be rid of her.

His fingers trailed lightly down her neck. "Did I ever tell you how big my bed is, how soft the mattress is?"

Her pulse raced at his words. Slowly, she lifted her gaze to meet his. "Why don't you just show me?"

"I intend to." He gazed at her mouth, let his fingers linger a moment longer on her neck, then stepped away. "You can count on it."

Two days later, they rode into the Circle B, tired and hungry. The sun hung low on the horizon, painting the distant clouds with streaks of pink and fiery gold. A warm breeze welcomed them, along with four of Sam's ranch hands who waved their hats and whistled from a large corral beside the barn. When they recognized the silver-haired man riding alongside their boss and his new wife, the hands all froze. Mouths dropped opened and eyes widened as they watched the trio of riders stop in front of the barn.

Everyone stared, including Gazella who'd run out to see what all the commotion was about. The plump housekeeper covered her mouth with both hands, then crossed herself and rambled excitedly in Spanish.

Sam helped Faith off her horse, then handed the reins to Clayton, his foreman.

"Welcome back, boss." With a hand as worn and leathered as his face, Clayton tipped his hat to Faith. "Mrs. McCants."

"Thank you." She offered a hesitant smile.

Though the farce no longer seemed necessary, Sam slipped an arm around Faith's shoulders and pulled her against him. He felt her stiffen, then saw her glance up at him in confusion. "I'd appreciate it if you'd take care of the horses, Clay. My wife and I would like to clean up and rest a little while before dinner."

"Sure thing, Boss. Be happy to."

Everyone else had crowded around Digger, slapping his back, asking questions all at the same time. Gazella tentatively touched Digger, discovered he wasn't a ghost, then, with a scream threw herself in his arms.

"Digger," Sam called over the ruckus. "We're going in. You coming?"

Digger waved them on, obviously enjoying the attention. Somehow the story that he'd told them about not even realizing there was a flood had evolved into a life-threatening close encounter with nature. Shaking his head, Sam pulled Faith with him into the kitchen, grabbed a box of cheesy crackers on their way through, and guided her up the stairs.

Then stopped in front of her bedroom.

She looked at the bedroom across the hall—*his* bedroom—then back to him. He smiled at her. "You've had a long day, Faith. Take a soak in the tub and get some rest."

Because he couldn't help himself, he pulled her against him and kissed her, long and hard. He let his lips linger, then reluctantly let her go. She leaned back against the door, her eyes soft and heavy, her lips still wet from his kiss.

It cost him not to reach for her again, not to drag her into his bedroom, into his bed, not to bury himself deep within her as he'd wanted to do for the past two days. But the shadows under her eyes and the weary slump of her shoulders told him she needed sleep. He wanted her, badly, but he wasn't an animal—though the feelings she evoked in him were not so far off.

"Rest up, sweetheart." He ran a finger over her soft cheek. "You're going to need it."

"Get some rest yourself, cowboy." She smiled slowly, seductively, then rose on her tiptoes and nipped his bottom lip as she ran her hands down his chest. "You're going to need it, too."

Still facing him, she opened the door and backed into the room. "Go ahead and keep the crackers."

The glint in her eye was wicked. "A little nourishment will keep up your...strength."

He had to remind himself to breathe after the door closed. On a groan, he dropped his head against the door jamb, then stumbled across the hall to his bedroom.

A shower was what he needed, he decided. A cold one.

With a smile still on her lips, Faith leaned against the other side of the door, then laughed softly when she heard Sam's groan. She felt exactly the same way.

The sound of laughter from outside caught her attention. She moved to the window, drew the lace curtain aside, and looked out. Digger sat on a tree stump beside the barn, animated by whatever story he was telling. Gazella perched on the edge of a watering trough beside him, while the ranch hands were all huddled around, hats tipped back, faces pressed forward, listening intently.

Smiling, she shook her head. Digger was going to play out his resurrection for all it was worth. And based on the rapt expressions on the faces of those in his audience, it was worth a considerable amount. After all, it wasn't every day that someone came back from the dead.

Especially her own father.

Her father. It had gotten easier over the past two days to say those words, though it still seemed strange to her. The only father she'd ever known was Joseph Courtland, but Joseph and Digger couldn't have been more opposite. Joseph had been highbrow, well-bred and proper. Digger was rugged, coarse and outlandish. Joseph had taught her propriety; Digger made her laugh.

Everything had been so clear to her before. She'd been lied to, manipulated. It was easy to be angry. Now she wasn't so sure. The past two days in Lonesome Rock Canyon had been a beginning for them, and though a bit rocky—she smiled at the pun—it was a start. She could understand what it was her mother had seen in Digger. He was full of life—bigger than life—energetic, unpretentious.

She smiled at that. He had enough money to buy a warehouse of Armani, but he wore old jeans and a patched woolen jacket. Some might call that eccentric, but now that she knew him, she understood he simply had a different perception of what was important in life. Money meant nothing to him. He was honest about who he was, what he was. He didn't give a damn what anyone else thought.

Except for Colleen Courtland. Faith knew that he loved her mother more than life itself; she saw it in his eyes every time he said her name. Whatever he'd done in the past, and even what he did now, she understood it was out of love for her mother. And for his daughter.

Whatever the past had been, whatever had happened, it was done. There was no changing it. She could accept it and move on, make her own life—or be bitter. The choice was hers.

And that fact reassured her. She was good at making decisions, wasn't she? Logically, calmly. Why should this situation be any different?

But it was, of course, she thought with a sigh. Not only because of Digger, but because of Sam. This was no longer a business deal, an unemotional transaction between two parties. Her heart was involved, and it hurt like hell.

She let the curtain fall back into place as she closed her eyes against the tears that threatened. How could she have let herself fall in love with Sam? And now that she had, how was she going to leave here, go back to Boston, and pretend that her life was the same as before?

She had no idea.

She hated this uncertainty, this confusion. She liked everything in order, not wild and reckless. Harold had never made her feel this way. Harold made her feel comfortable. Secure. Safe.

Sam was definitely not safe.

Drawing in a deep breath, she turned and headed for the bathroom, wondering if cold showers really did work.

When the cold spray did nothing to ease the fire inside him, Sam flipped the faucet to hot, placed both palms on the hunter-green tile and dropped his head under the shower head.

Maybe he could drown himself.

The hot water beat on his neck and shoulders, slowly melting the tension, the frustration, the desperation.

It wasn't enough.

Eyes closed, the roar of water pounding his head, he let his mind wander to the woman across the hall. He tried not to think about the fact that she would be leaving soon. Too soon.

And why wouldn't she? She'd married him—and

he'd married her—for personal gain. There'd been no words of love, no promise of forever. Digger's return cancelled the marriage, and they both had what they wanted.

Didn't they?

He'd watched her the past two days, listened as she and Digger took the first tentative steps toward a relationship. She'd been cautious, kept the conversation superficial—business mostly—careful not to enter into territory that was too personal or too intimate. But slowly, he'd seen her loosen up, smile, even laugh, at Digger's exuberance.

It had taken tremendous restraint for him to keep his distance from her, to keep his hands off her. Especially when he'd seen her watching him, too, her gaze openly seductive, promising. But they both knew that they would have to bide their time until they got back to the ranch, where they could be alone, behind a closed door.

He pulled his head out from under the faucet, then swept his drenched hair off his face. He'd always considered himself a patient man, but when it came to Faith, nothing was clear anymore. Nothing felt sure. Somehow she'd eased her way into his life, gotten under his skin. He had no idea how to deal with the feelings she evoked in him. Feelings he'd never had before, for any woman.

He didn't just want her in his bed, dammit. He wanted her in his life.

At the sound of the shower door opening, he whipped his head around. She stood there—this woman who haunted his every thought—wearing a long, floral robe. He saw the hesitation in her eyes, the nervous tug of her teeth on her bottom lip.

"I couldn't sleep." Her hands loosened the belt of her robe. It fell open and slid slowly off her smooth shoulders, down her slender body, over her long, long legs, then pooled at her feet. "I thought maybe a shower would relax me."

His heart tripped at the sight of her standing in front of him, gloriously naked, cheeks flushed, hair swirling around her bare shoulders. Need clawed at his insides; blood pounded in his temples. He reached for her, pulled her into the large shower stall with him.

"Think again, sweetheart."

Ten

He dragged her against him, pressed her back against the cool tile, covered her mouth with his. Water sluiced over her body, her shoulders, her breasts, and glistened on her smooth, silky skin. His hands followed the path of the water, kneaded each rosy-peaked breast, moved across her narrow waist and flat belly, then lowered to the juncture of her thighs. She gasped and moved against him as he caressed her intimately, dipping into the moist heat of her body. Her soft, low moan ripped through him like wildfire.

Her head fell back limply as he trailed kisses over her neck, all the while stroking her, arousing and pleasing not only her, but himself, as well. She was so small under his large, rough hands. So soft and hot. When she trembled beneath him, his control snapped.

He gripped her buttocks tightly, lifted her and buried himself deeply inside her.

Her arms came tightly around his neck. She strained against him, quivered in his arms. He lunged wildly into her, again and again. She shuddered uncontrollably, bit into his shoulder to muffle her cry. He drove himself inside her, and felt the pain—the pleasure—rip him apart, empty him. On a deep, guttural groan, he pressed his face into her wet, slick neck.

Weak, his breath ragged, he lowered her, then gathered her in his arms and pulled her close again.

Feeling as if her knees might give way, Faith looped her arms around Sam's neck. Steam swirled around them, creating an ethereal effect. Water pounded the tile floor, splashed on their feet and legs.

"I can't move," she said breathlessly.

"You don't have to." He reached for the soap, turned it over in his hands several times, then slowly started rubbing her body.

She lost all sense of time. Minutes or hours might have passed. Her eyes drifted closed as he worked his magic over her. His hands slid over her wet skin, massaged and stroked. Her breathing deepened with each dip of his fingers. Her heart, barely recovered from his last assault, began to pound again.

They sank to the floor of the large shower stall, and he pulled her on top of him, then caught her hips and lifted her onto him. She moved over him, ran her hands over the slick, hard muscles of his arms and chest, lost herself in the primitive rhythm of love.

That rhythm built until it became as frenzied, as urgent as before. His fingers dug into her hips and she bowed backward, slid her hands upward over her wet body. His voice raw, he murmured both endearments and curses. Sensations tightened and knotted inside her, low in her belly, lower still, until the pleasure turned to pain and release was the only escape.

With a harsh cry and a muffled groan, they escaped together.

They bundled up in towels and robes, and he carried her to his bed, stretching his long body next to hers. She ran a hand over the thick, chocolate-brown comforter, and a sense of belonging overwhelmed her. A sense of completeness. How could she ever have known she would find it here—with this man?

Hair wrapped in a towel, she laid her head on his shoulder, snuggled deeper into his arms. He brushed his lips against her forehead and pulled her closer.

"You're right. This is a big bed."

He smiled softly. "Much too big for one person."

"Two people is just right," she said in her best Goldilocks impersonation. She watched his eyes as he stared intently at her in the dim light of the bedside table.

"Stay with me, Faith."

The words slipped out of Sam's mouth without any thought behind them. Watching her, here, in his bed beside him, he only knew what he felt...what he needed. He needed her.

She touched his cheek, smiled softly. "I'm not going anywhere."

He covered her hand with his and shook his head. "I mean, stay with me. Don't go back to Boston. You'd made plans to stay for two months, anyway. So stay."

Surprise flared in her eyes. ‘‘I...I don’t know what to say.’’

‘‘Don’t say anything right now. Think about it. Think about this.’’ He kissed her tenderly, slowly. ‘‘And while you’re thinking, I’m going to go round us up some food. You’re right—’’ he said, brushing his lips over hers ‘‘—I am going to need to keep up my strength.’’

She laughed softly, dragged one of his pillows close to her and hugged it. ‘‘Hurry.’’

‘‘Don’t worry about that.’’ He dressed quickly, hungry already for more than food. A hunger he worried might never be appeased.

The house was quiet and dark, and he realized that Gazella had left already. Digger was most likely out at the bunkhouse with Clay and the men, spinning tales and basking in all the attention, Sam thought with a shake of his head. He took a minute to go over the mail piled on the entry table, dismissed the bulk of it, then made his way to the kitchen.

And found Digger rooting through the refrigerator. Arms loaded with bowls of fried chicken, potato salad and green beans, he booted the refrigerator closed, then deposited his cache on the counter.

‘‘Sammy.’’ Digger pulled out a chicken leg. ‘‘Just in time to eat.’’

Sam moved into the kitchen, leaned back against the counter, arms folded. ‘‘I’ll take a plate up. It’s been a long day.’’

‘‘A long several days, eh, son?’’ Grinning, Digger spooned potato salad onto a plate. ‘‘How’s that girl of mine?’’

‘‘Tired.’’ Though not just from the mountain trip,

he thought, and forced back the threatening smile. "You've put her through a lot, Digger."

Nodding, Digger sighed, spooned green beans beside the potato salad, then dropped another chicken leg on the plate. "She's a tough one, Sammy. Bounces right back. Last year, when Elijah Jane lost the Holden's Market account, our largest retail distributors for frozen food, Faith single-handedly went after Holden's main competition and negotiated a deal for nearly double."

He chuckled as he sat at the kitchen table. "Thirty years ago, all I'd ever done in my life was a little cowpoking and some mining. I never intended to be in the restaurant business. If that bastard Leo hadn't run out on me, I never would have been. Surprised myself to find out I was good at it. All I ever intended to do was recoup my money and sell the place, but then I fell in love." He smiled and shook his head. "Digger Jones. Head-over-heels in love with a lady. And the damnedest part was she loved me, too."

He stared at the food on his plate, but didn't touch it. "It nearly killed me when I found out she married another man. I went a little crazy for a while. When I finally found out the truth, Faith was already born. I couldn't believe it. Me. A papa. Damned if that wasn't the happiest and most miserable day of my life all at the same time." His voice caught, wavered for a moment before he cleared his throat. "I only saw her once, when she was six months old...but I loved that little girl more than life itself."

Sam had never seen this tender, open side of Digger before. He hadn't even known it existed. "But

Elijah Jane,'' he asked quietly, ''you kept it, expanded again and again. Why?''

''For Faith.'' He looked at Sam, his blue eyes sharp and clear. ''Everything was for Faith. I had to have something to give her, something that was more than money. Something that was not only a part of me, but that she was a part of, too. Her mama and I kept in touch over the years, but only through the mail. She arranged for Faith to get a summer job at Elijah Jane, but nothing was ever handed to her. No one in the company knew she was my daughter. She worked her butt off and earned every promotion all on her own.''

''But if it's hers...'' Sam asked, ''...if you'd always intended it to be hers, why didn't you just give it to her? Why all this nonsense about marrying me?''

Digger gestured to the chair across from him, then sighed when Sam sat down. ''I watched my little girl grow up from a distance,'' he said quietly. ''Sometimes her mama would send me a snapshot of her, or occasionally a picture she'd drawn. It was all I ever had of her. But even from a distance, I always knew she'd be something special. Damn if I wasn't right.'' He beamed, then shook his head. ''Problem was, she's just too damn stubborn for her own good.''

Sam gave a snort of laughter. Not that he didn't agree, but to hear those words out of Digger's mouth seemed ludicrous.

Digger frowned at him. ''Don't you go laughing at me, boy. I admit I'm a mite set in my ways, but I'm always open to reason.''

''About as open as the post office at midnight.'' Sam's sarcasm earned him a hard look. ''That's why you forced her to marry me if she wanted Elijah Jane, 'cause you're so open-minded.''

Digger's frown deepened. ''She was gonna marry that accountant fellow. An accountant, for crying out loud. He's all wrong for her—she's just too headstrong to see it right now. You, on the other hand, are just right. I knew if I gave you and Faith a nudge, you'd hit it off.''

''A nudge?'' Sam rolled his eyes. ''I'd say getting married is more like a body slam, Digger.''

He stabbed at the potato salad, took a healthy bite. ''I will admit I was feeling a little desperate with Faith's wedding getting so close and all.''

''Desperate enough to fake your own death?''

Digger went still, then very slowly lowered his fork. ''Fake my death?'' he repeated evenly. ''What kind of nonsense is that?''

''It never made any sense to me, not even from the beginning, when you were first missing.'' Sam picked up a chicken thigh, bit into it, then settled back in his chair. ''You knew those mountains like nobody else, survived all kinds of weather, even escaped with a broken leg that time you fell down the shaft. You always came out all right. Digger Jones was too tough to be bested by Mother Nature.''

He paused, waiting for Digger to say something, but the old man was silent. ''But two months was a hell of a long time. If you'd said two weeks, day fourteen you were always back. The flood was an extra stroke of luck for you, wasn't it? It wiped out your camp and you knew everyone would think you'd drowned.''

''Can't help what folks think,'' Digger grumbled.

"It's what you *wanted* us to think, Digger. You had to be dead in order for your little plan to work. You'd disappear in the mountains...we'd all think you were dead...I'd read the will...and Faith and I would marry to get the carrots you dangled. So tell me, was Faith's mother in on this, too?"

Digger straightened, his mouth pinched at the corners. "Colleen doesn't know a thing, and don't you go saying nothing 'bout her neither or I'll have to—"

Digger stopped suddenly, realizing that he'd said too much already. When Sam raised his eyebrows, Digger leaned back in his chair and shook his head slowly. "Just one of the things I like about you, Sammy. You're smart, always looking past the surface—unlike most folks. So tell me, how long have you known?"

"Three days." Sam took another bite of chicken. "Probably since about ten minutes after you strolled into the mining camp. You were much too casual, and much too agreeable, especially after you found out that Faith and I got married. Digger Jones is neither casual, nor agreeable."

"I can be just as agreeable as the next fellow," Digger complained.

"Yeah, if the next person is Attila the Hun," Sam returned.

"Don't you smart-mouth me, Sam McCants. I'll whup you so hard that—" He stopped, then sighed heavily. "So the burning question is, what are you gonna tell Faith?"

"That's a good question, Sam. I'd like to hear the answer myself."

Both men looked up abruptly. Faith stood in the

kitchen doorway, dressed in her robe, her hair wet and combed back from her pale face. Lips pressed tightly together, she stared at Digger.

Damn.

One careful step at a time, she moved into the kitchen, her bare feet soundless on the oak floor. "Well, now, look here. Cold chicken. What an appropriate meal for the two of you."

"Faith." Sam stood slowly, his eyes sheepish as he met her gaze. "How long have you been standing there?"

Smiling, Faith shoved her hands into the pockets of her robe. "Long enough. Why don't you sit back down, Sam? In fact, I think I'll join you. I'm starving."

She sat at the table, reached for a piece of chicken, even took a bite. It was tender and juicy, but it might as well have been a slice of cardboard. Sam slowly sat, his eyes still focused on her.

"Faith, don't—"

"You haven't answered Digger's question." Her words were so calm, she even surprised herself. "Is there something you have to tell me?"

"Faith." Digger's voice was quiet, his tone imploring. "This is between you and me. Let's talk about it, just us, and leave Sammy out of it."

"I wouldn't dream of leaving *Sammy* out of it. After all, he is my *husband,* isn't he?" She took another bite of chicken, chewed slowly, carefully, and prayed she wouldn't gag as she swallowed. "Isn't trust and communication what every good marriage is based on?"

Sam's jaw clenched tight as he stared at her, but he said nothing.

"Don't be mad at Sam." Digger sighed. "I'm the only one you should be mad at here."

"Who said I was mad?" Deep inside, there were emotions swirling—dark, heavy emotions. But outside, she felt only numb, as if she'd been out in the freezing cold way too long.

She looked at Digger, struggled to keep her voice even. "Why should one more lie from you—from anyone—make a difference to me? The fact is, this is business. It's always been business. What we have here is a win-win situation. You got what you wanted, which was for me to marry Sam. Sam got his land. I got Elijah Jane. In fact, we should be celebrating a successful deal." She dropped her chicken onto a plate, then brushed off her hands. "You have any champagne, Sam?"

"Faith, honey, I only wanted what was best for you." Digger leaned toward her and reached for her hand, but she stood quickly.

"Just like my grandfather wanted what was best for my mother." She saw him wince, knew that her arrow had hit its mark. "Why do you think you're any different from him? What he did was wrong, and what you did was wrong. You can't manipulate other people's lives, Digger, no matter how good you think your intentions are. But to plan your own death, to let all your friends—people who care about you—think you were dead, that's unforgivable."

"I never wanted to hurt you, honey." Digger stood, his gaze somber. "You have to believe that."

She pulled at the belt on her robe, drew in a deep

breath, closed her eyes, then opened them again. "In your own way, I know you meant well. But whatever decisions I make, whatever mistakes—" she said, glancing at Sam, then back to Digger "—they have to be my own. If you and I are ever going to have any kind of relationship, you're going to have to accept that."

"I will, honey." Digger nodded, and had the decency to lower his eyes. "I swear. Just give me a chance, I won't let you down."

She managed to smile at that, knowing the difficulty he would have keeping his word. "I'm glad you're alive, Digger. I'm even glad we've met. But I need some time, some distance, to think about where we go from here. I'm going back to Boston tomorrow. We can talk again in a few days."

She had no idea how she managed to walk away without her knees giving out, but somehow she made it through the kitchen, the entry, and was halfway up the stairs when Sam caught her arm and spun her around.

"We need to talk about this," he said tightly.

"You knew three days ago that all this was nothing more than a sham." She prayed her voice wouldn't crack, that the touch of his hand on her arm wouldn't send her sinking to her knees. "Why didn't you tell me, Sam?"

"I needed to talk with Digger first, hear what he had to say."

"And then were you going to tell me the truth?"

His hand tightened on her arm. "Faith, I know how you must feel, but—"

"No. You don't know anything about how I feel. Were you going to tell me?"

Eyes narrowed, jaw clenched tight, he looked into her eyes. "I don't know."

"Well, at least that's honest." She rubbed at the ache in her temple, but it was the ache in her heart that truly hurt. "I'm tired, Sam. I'm going to bed."

"Come with me." He pulled her closer to him. "I don't want you to be alone."

It would be so easy to give in, to let him take her in his arms, into his bed. She could lose herself there, maybe even forget for a little while that she'd been lied to, made a fool of.

"I just want you to know that...that I don't regret our time together. You've had your life thrown into an upheaval because of me...because Digger had some misguided belief that we belonged together. But everything that we had was based on a lie," she said quietly, her cheeks burning. "It doesn't matter that Digger meant well. It was still just smoke and mirrors, an illusion. It was a fantasy."

She stepped away from him and slipped the ring he had given her off her finger. He winced as she pressed it into his hand.

"But this is reality, Sam. I need to go back to Boston, to Elijah Jane. You need to be here."

He stared at the ring, then closed his hand around it. "Our marriage was legal, Faith," he said quietly. "You're still my wife."

His words surprised her. She looked at him, but couldn't read his eyes. What was he saying? Was he simply reminding her that they had unfinished business—that the marriage needed to be annulled?

Dammit, why couldn't she read what was in his heart?

"I—I'll have my lawyer handle it when I get back to Boston." She forced a light tone to her voice. "Consider yourself a single man, Sam. Free to do whatever you like, with whomever you like."

His face was like granite, his eyes empty. He stared at her for a long moment, then stepped away. "Gazella will be here in the morning. If you need anything, just ask her."

"Thank you." How was it possible to be so polite, so civil, when a scream was so close to the surface? "Good night, then. I'll see you in the morning."

"'Fraid not. I have work to catch up on. I'll be gone early."

"Oh. Well, goodbye, then." She stuck her hand out.

Something in his eyes flared. He reached for her with blinding speed, pulled her into his arms and covered her mouth with his, smothering her gasp. He kissed her roughly, a kiss that made her feel her bones were melting.

He released her just as suddenly, and turned before she could regain her breath.

He never even looked back.

Eleven

"What do you think, Mom, the pearled scoop neck I just had on, or this one?"

The dress was satin, with a heart-shaped lace bodice, full skirt and long, tight lace sleeves. As she moved, the fabric shimmered under the dressing room's soft fluorescent lights, and the large diamond engagement ring on her finger winked. Her mother, busy unbuttoning the sleeves of a chiffon and crepe dress hanging in the corner, did not acknowledge her daughter's question.

"Mom, the shop is on fire, and they've asked that we exit in an orderly manner."

Colleen glanced up and blinked. "That's nice, dear. Lovely."

Faith sighed and in a rustle of thick underskirts turned to face her mother. "You want to tell me where you were?"

Colleen's brow furrowed. "Where I was?"

"Just now. All week, for that matter. Ever since we started shopping for the wedding."

Colleen unfastened the last button and fluffed the crepe skirt. "I have no idea what you mean."

Slipping an arm around her mother's shoulders, Faith turned so they both faced the mirror. Colleen's hair was a shade darker than Faith's and threaded with silver, but their features were nearly identical. Only the eyes were so very different. Colleen's spring green and Faith's pale blue.

Digger's eyes.

"You know exactly what I mean," Faith said. "You've been quiet—too quiet—for the past four weeks, ever since I got back from Texas. You've lost weight, you're not smiling, and you've got dark circles under your eyes."

Colleen glanced into the mirror and frowned. "How unkind of you to mention that. But while we're on the subject, dear, I believe those are the exact words I intended to say to you."

It was Faith's turn to frown. It was true. She hadn't been eating; she'd been cranky; and makeup just wasn't working on the shadows under her eyes. "There's been a lot to catch up on since I got back from Texas. Reports, board meetings, the new Meyer's account. I've been a little busy."

"I heard Wade Thornton's been handling Meyer's beautifully," Colleen said. "He also filled in for you very well while you were gone."

"See what happens when I'm gone too long? The competition moves in. Wade covets the executive washroom. And anyway, we're not talking about me, we're talking about you."

"*I'm* talking about *you,*" Colleen said quietly. "I spoke with Digger again last night."

Faith dropped her arm and fidgeted with the dress. "You've spoken to him quite a bit."

"He's worried about you. You left so angry."

"Of course I left angry." And every time she reminded herself that she had every right to be furious with him, all she could see was the pain in his eyes when she'd said goodbye. "He lied to me, forced me to marry Sam. Manipulated me."

"He loves you, dear." Colleen zipped up the dress Faith had on and gazed soulfully at her daughter in the mirror. "Perhaps his intentions were a little misguided, but he was so certain that you and Sam would be right for each other."

Sam. Every time she thought the ache in her heart might ease, that just maybe she might get through one day, one hour even, without the pain of his memory ripping her insides apart, he was there again. In her thoughts, in her heart, in her soul. She could see him so clearly; his heart-stopping smile, his deep, sexy eyes. Charming one minute, arrogant the next. And as a lover...gentle, and so incredibly and wonderfully skilled.

Not a night had passed in four weeks that she hadn't awakened, her body aching for his touch. He hadn't called, not even once. And though she'd reached for the phone dozens of times, pride forced her to hang up.

"This is the nineties, Mom. Arranged marriages don't work." Faith stared at her reflection in the mirror. Brides were supposed to glow—not glower. "You of all people should know that."

Colleen's startled expression stared back at Faith in the mirror. Shocked at her own lack of grace, Faith pressed a hand to her mouth. "Oh, Mom, I'm so sorry. I didn't mean that."

"Your father—Joseph—was a good man. A hard worker, always made sure that you and I had the best of everything." She touched Faith's hair, tucked it behind her ear, then sighed. "But it's true. I never loved him."

"I had no right to say that." Faith hugged her mother. "I know you did what was best for me."

"I wasn't a strong woman, sweetheart. I gave in to pressure from my parents…and married without love." There was so much emotion in her mother's eyes, and so much that Faith was certain she didn't know. "I almost left him one year later. I'd even packed our things. I was willing to give up everything for Digger—everything except you. When Joseph threatened a custody battle, I was too frightened to leave."

"But what about later," Faith insisted, "when I was older, and Digger had money to fight for you? Why didn't he come for you then?"

Colleen brushed a stray curl from Faith's forehead. "Digger was working his mine, running his café. That's where he belonged. His life was the complete opposite of ours…and he had too much pride to ask me to come to Texas, to give up my life in Boston and be with him. I was certain he didn't love me anymore, and I had too much pride to go to him."

Colleen touched her daughter's cheek. "But pride

is a lonely companion. I made a mistake twenty-seven years ago, Faith. A woman should never marry a man she doesn't love. Especially if she's in love with someone else.''

A chill curled through Faith. Why did she have the feeling her mother was no longer talking about herself and Digger?

Did her mother know? she wondered. Were her feelings for Sam so obvious?

No, she told herself firmly. It wasn't Sam she wanted. It was Harold. Hadn't he calmly accepted her marriage to Sam, told her he'd understood and forgiven her?

Sam was all wrong for her. He might have his moments of charm, but he was argumentative, chauvinistic and overbearing. He'd never wanted to be married, he'd simply wanted the land, just as she'd wanted Elijah Jane. For him, their relationship had been physical. Sex. If he'd wanted anything more, he would have called.

Wouldn't he?

Dammit. Why hadn't he called?

Pride is a lonely companion.

The dress—a perfect fit only moments ago—now squeezed at her breasts and pinched at her waist. But it wasn't just the dress that suddenly felt too tight, she realized. It was her life.

''Faith.'' Colleen took her daughter by the arms. ''I have something to tell you. Please don't be upset.''

The serious tone in her mother's voice frightened her. ''Are you all right?''

''I'm getting married.''

The words didn't quite register. Faith stared at her mother, dumbfounded.

"I'm leaving Boston, sweetheart. I'm going to go to Texas and ask Digger to marry me. Beg if I have to. When I found out he wasn't dead...that he hadn't drowned in the mountains...what I needed to do became crystal clear. I love him. I always have. I lost my dream twenty-seven years ago, but I've been given a second chance. Whatever time we have—and knowing Digger, I suspect it will be a great many years—I'm going to spend with him."

"But your house, your friends at the club—"

"Joseph's friends, not mine. And I've already rented out the house with an option to sell. I'm leaving tomorrow."

"Tomorrow?" Desperate, confused, Faith swallowed back the tears in her throat. "But, you can't just leave. What will I do without you?"

"You'll be fine, dear. You have Elijah Jane now, and of course, Harold. What else do you need?"

Harold. Elijah Jane. Her hands began to shake and her knees threatened to fold.

What else did she need?

"That is what you wanted, isn't it, Faith?" her mother asked quietly, carefully studying her face. "Elijah Jane and Harold?"

"I...yes. Yes, of course. You've just caught me off guard, that's all." Forcing a smile, she kissed her mother quickly, then reached for the buttons at her wrists. The dressing room was closing in on her. She had to get out of this dress. "I'll take the rest of the day off. We'll go celebrate."

"He hasn't said yes, yet." With a smug smile, Colleen unzipped Faith's dress. "But he will. By God, he will."

Her mother's voice was adamant, her eyes shining with purpose. This was a side of Colleen Courtland that Faith had never seen, hadn't even realized existed and Faith looked at her as if she were seeing her for the first time. Her love for Digger had made her strong. Determined and tenacious. Even more beautiful than she already was.

Her mother knew what she wanted, and she was going after it.

Maybe it was time, Faith realized, to decide what it was that she really wanted, what she really needed for herself—and go after it, too.

Digger Jones was getting married.

The aisles in the church were packed to standing room only. After all, it wasn't often a person went to a man's funeral one month, his wedding the next. And besides that, Francis Elijah Montgomery—still just plain old Digger Jones to the town of Cactus Flat—getting married to a Boston socialite was an event that one had to see to believe.

Flowers. Organist. Candles. Digger in a black tuxedo.

Sam was seeing it all, and he still couldn't believe it.

"Wipe that stupid grin off your face, Sammy," Digger growled as he moved beside him. "Else I'll have to dirty up that penguin suit you got on."

"Now is that any way to speak to your best man? Smile for the camera, Digger. Savannah Stone's taking your picture."

Digger glared at the sudden flash. The Stone family occupied the entire two front rows in the church. Even Annie and Jared's four-week-old baby girl, Francine Elizabeth Stone—named in honor of Digger—was in attendance. Yawning, the baby snuggled deeper into her proud papa's arms.

A pressure built in his chest as he watched Annie press a kiss to Jared's cheek, as she gazed into her husband's eyes with a look that most men would go an entire life without seeing.

Sam frowned. Strange. He'd never envied his friends their marital happiness before. Admired maybe, but never envied.

Damn Faith Courtland. Before she'd come along, he'd been quite content—more than content, he corrected—*happy* with his life just as it had been. Footloose, free to come and go as he pleased. No one to answer to or argue with; no one to worry about.

Now, he sure as hell wasn't content, and he sure as hell wasn't happy.

He was in love.

He'd denied it the first few days she'd been gone. Told himself he just wanted what he couldn't have. The news had spread quickly, of course, that Sam McCants's bride had left him after only a few short days of marriage, and he'd endured the looks of pity and sympathetic pats on the back. Fortunately for him, Digger's return had overshadowed all other topics of gossip. There had been several phone calls, though, from lady friends, offering condolences and…comfort. He had turned them all down.

He'd received the annulment papers one week after she'd left. He'd picked up the phone—torn between raging at her and begging her to come back—slammed down the phone and then gotten good and drunk. He paid for it the next day, then repeated the process all over again the next night. Only this time he broke the phone and put his fist through a wall.

She was going to marry Arnold. There was nothing he could do about it. He'd even seen the announcement of their wedding date in a Boston newspaper that Digger had "accidentally" left lying on the counter in the café.

He'd punched his truck radio over that little bit of news. Now he had not only a crack in his dashboard, but a radio that didn't work.

Little Miss Calm-and-Composed would have gotten a big laugh out of that one.

He folded his arms and knew he was scowling, but didn't care. So let her marry Howard. Who the hell cared?

Technically, though, Sam thought, she was still married to him. For at least another two weeks. Assuming she'd be here today, at her own mother and father's wedding, he'd intended to get her alone and remind her of that fact. But she wasn't coming, Colleen had told him. Some nonsense about a corporate crisis.

So much for his fantasy that she would see him again, throw herself into his arms and admit she'd made a huge mistake—that she loved *him,* not that jerk she was engaged to.

But he'd had too many fantasies as it was this past month. Lack of sleep and sheets ripped from the bed every morning were testament to that. Dreams haunted him: images of her soft blue eyes, her sweet mouth, her baby-smooth skin.

One night, when he couldn't sleep, he'd even made the mistake of watching a copy of the video Jared had given him of Faith holding Madeline at Jake's house. He'd watched her playing with the little girl, laughing and honking, and he'd ached for her. For the sound of her voice, the sight of that stubborn little chin lifting in defiance, the feel of her body next to his.

Damn! How he still missed her…wanted her.

And that knowledge only made him mad as hell.

Sam glanced over at Carol Sue in the third row. She was batting her thick eyelashes at him, smiling at him like a fisherman who'd just spotted a big bass.

It made him even more furious that he wasn't remotely interested.

"You got the ring?" Digger glanced nervously at his watch, put his hands into his pockets, took them out again.

"In my pocket."

"Where's that damned photographer?"

"She's with Colleen, in the dressing room."

"Did you sign the wedding certificate?"

Sam smiled at the bead of perspiration on Digger's forehead. He'd been the typical bridegroom all week: anxious, nervous as hell and beaming every time Colleen's name was mentioned. "I thought we signed the certificate *after* the ceremony."

Digger shook his head. "Before."

"All right." The organist droned out "With Thine Eyes," and Sam could have sworn Digger paled. "I'll be right back."

Reverend Winslow's office was empty, and remarkably quiet considering the buzz of people and music out in the church. An overhead fan stirred the warm air in the closed office and ruffled the papers on his large oak desk. Sam spotted the certificate on the desk, patted his pocket, then plucked a ballpoint pen from the reverend's desktop penholder.

He started to sign his name, then froze at the sight of the name already penned neatly beside his. Faith McCants.

He stared at the signature, then frowned. How could Faith be a witness? She wasn't even here.

He looked at the signature again. She *was* here. She had to be if she'd signed her name.

His hand tightened around the pen in his fingers. He took a deep breath to calm himself, afraid he might run out into the church like some kind of madman to search the crowd. That he'd tell her right there, in front of the entire church full of people that he wasn't letting her go, that she *was* his wife—in every way—and she better damn well get used to it.

That ought to go over real well, he thought miserably.

"Hello, Sam."

He whirled at the sound of Faith's voice behind him. She stood in the open doorway.

Too stunned to speak, he simply stared.

She had on the pretty lace dress she'd worn for their own wedding. Her hair was pulled up; curls shimmered around her flushed face. A small pearl necklace circled her slender neck. She looked beautiful.

"Faith." He told himself to be calm, to be cool.

He racked his brain for something clever to say. ''So you made it to the wedding.''

Oh, that was good. Real clever.

''I didn't think I should miss my mother and father getting married, especially after twenty-seven years.'' She closed the door behind her, then leaned back against it, holding a manila folder against her stomach. ''How are you, Sam?''

His first instinct was to drag her into his arms and show her exactly how he felt. But first instincts were much too dangerous right now. ''Fine,'' he said tightly. ''Just fine. And you?''

''Fine.'' Her gaze, steady only a moment ago, dropped slightly. ''I saw Jared and Annie's baby last night. She's beautiful.''

''Yeah.'' She had been in town since last night and hadn't come to see him? A knot formed in his gut, an ache in his chest. Jaw clenched, he turned away and signed his name.

''I'd thought you might call,'' she said quietly.

In spite of his vow to be calm, to face her without letting her know his heart was bleeding, he couldn't turn off the sudden flash of anger. How could she walk in here so composed, so unruffled and casually ask him why he hadn't called?

Very carefully, he laid the pen on the desk, then moved toward her. ''When did you think I might call? To return *your* phone call...a call you never made?''

''I was going—''

''Or maybe when I read you and Howard had set the date.'' He felt the frustration pour through him. ''Or maybe even when I received the annulment papers from you. You wouldn't have wanted me to call then, Faith. Trust me on that one.''

''Sam, if you'd—''

''What the hell is it you want from me?'' He was in her face now, only inches from her, struggling to keep his hands off her, to keep from dragging her into his arms. ''To be phone buddies? Exchange birthday or Christmas cards? You can just damn well forget that. I'm not Arnold, and I'm sure as hell not understanding.''

''Sam, please!'' She'd raised her voice, a rare occurrence for Faith Courtland. When she had his attention, her voice softened again. ''I want to talk to you about the annulment.''

An ice-cold chill settled in his stomach as he watched her pull an envelope out of her folder. She'd brought the papers for him to sign. Rage filled him. Rage and love and a desperation that had him shaking.

He'd fight the annulment tooth and nail. Maybe she'd come here only because of her mother's wedding, but there was no way in hell he was letting her go again. She was his, dammit.

''You want to talk about the annulment? Fine. Let's talk about it.'' He strode evenly across the room, took the envelope out of her hand, tore it in half, then handed it back to her. ''End of discussion. I'm not signing the damn papers.''

Eyes wide, she stared at the ripped envelope, then glanced back up at him. ''It wasn't necessary to tear them up, Sam.''

''Yes, dammit, it was. Very necessary. I'm not going to let you marry Howard.'' Sam suddenly had a thought. ''Is he here? Let me tell him, myself.'' He welcomed the opportunity—relished it. His hands tightened into fists.

''Oh, for heaven's sake.'' She rolled her eyes. ''I'm trying to tell you, none of this is necessary.''

At her patient tone, something inside him snapped. He needed to shake her up, to see her lose that damn control of hers. To make her feel just a little of what he was feeling.

He pushed her back against the door and crushed his mouth down on hers. Satisfaction flooded through him when she melted into him. Her soft whimper had him pulling her tighter to him, deepening the kiss, moving over her lips with all the hunger—all the need—that had been building in him over the past few weeks.

''Sam. Stop.'' She pressed a hand to his chest. ''I want you to read something.''

''I never read and kiss at the same time,'' he murmured, moving over her neck, remembering that sensitive spot behind her ear. ''It's not normally considered polite.''

She shivered, then stiffened and pushed against him. ''Sam. I want you to read this. Now.''

With a sigh, he let go of her. She thrust a Boston newspaper at him. The society pages. He froze at the picture at the top of the page.

It was Faith. She was smiling, standing beside some guy who looked like he belonged on the cover of *GQ*. Wasn't it bad enough he had to know she wanted to marry another guy? Did he have to see it in black and white, too?

He grabbed the paper intending to rip it to shreds as he had the annulment papers, then caught the last half of the headline.

...Engagement Called Off.

Snapping the paper open, he skimmed urgently to absorb the article.

> Harold Peterson...Faith Courtland...announced yesterday...no explanations...Ms. Courtland also announced her intended leave of absence from her newly appointed position as president of Elijah Jane Corporation.

Numb, he looked at her. A small smile played around her lips. Lips still moist from his kiss. "You called off your engagement?"

She nodded.

Eyes narrowed, he moved in closer. "And you let me go on like that?"

"*I* let you go on?" Laughter bubbled out of her.

It was bad enough he had made a fool of himself. Now she was laughing at him, too. A man could only take so much. To release his frustration, and because those lips of hers were so damn tempting, he yanked her to him and kissed her again.

How in the world were they supposed to have a conversation if he kept kissing her like this? Faith thought dimly. There was so much she wanted to say to him, to tell him.

Blood pounded in her head, blocking out the organ music and muffled voices from the wedding guests. All she knew was Sam: the heady scent of his aftershave, the hard, insistent press of his mouth against hers, the incredibly arousing play of his hands on her neck, her arms, her waist. How she'd missed this... wanted this...wanted him.

She'd been terrified to walk in here, not certain how he felt about her, or if he'd turn her away. She'd risked everything: her pride, her heart. But it hadn't mattered. All that mattered was Sam.

But when those hands moved upward again, bracketing her rib cage, and his thumbs skimmed the soft underside of her breasts, she gasped and pulled away. "There's a wedding about to take place," she said breathlessly.

His eyes, hooded with desire, suddenly flashed at her. "Tell me why you called off your engagement."

She met his look and held it. "You know why."

He shook his head. "You tell me."

"My mother convinced me it was wrong to marry someone I didn't love." She leaned back against the door, drew in a shaky breath. "Especially when I'm in love with someone else."

He waited, his gaze boring into her.

"I'm in love with you, Sam."

There. She'd said it. And it hadn't been nearly as difficult as she'd anticipated during the entire flight over.

"I think I loved you from the beginning," she said softly. "At least from the time you fed me chocolate cake." He raised an eyebrow at her teasing. "You made me laugh," she went on, running a hand up the lapel of his tuxedo, "made me furious. Made me feel. More than I wanted to, more than I'd ever allowed myself to. Control was my only defense against being hurt, but I had no control with you. Not emotionally, not physically.''

Her cheeks heated at her blatant admission, but she was in too deep now. Just as she had felt in the raging river in which she had nearly died, she was helpless, powerless to stop what was happening. The only difference was, this time she didn't want to stop it. This time, it would save her—not destroy her.

''You upset my life...my heart. And that was the one thing that scared me the most. I was certain I'd lose *me* if I let myself love you.'' She touched his cheek, then brushed her lips against his. ''Instead, I found myself.''

He pressed his brow to hers. ''And Harold?''

Faith sighed, leaned into him. ''I think he was relieved, though he was too much of a gentleman to admit it. He wished me well, wished *us* well, actually.''

Sam arched a brow at that, then glanced down at the envelope in her hands.

She handed him back the envelope he had ripped in two. ''Look inside.''

He did, and found small shreds of paper inside the torn envelope. When he looked at her in surprise, she smiled. ''I told you it wasn't necessary to tear them up. I already had. I love you, Sam. If you want me, if you let me stay, I'll show you how much.''

''If I *let* you stay? Good God, woman, I was ready to tie you up and drag you back with me. There's no way I am going to let you get away from me again. I love you, sweetheart. I want you to stay and be my wife. Really be my wife. The mother of my children.''

A real marriage. Children.

She snuggled in his arms, too happy, too content to speak.

"This leave of absence—" he said as he kissed her cheek, her nose "—how much time do we have? Before you have to go back to Boston, back to Elijah Jane? We're going to have to come up with some kind of arrangement to commute after your leave is up, but in the meantime, I don't want to waste one minute."

She cupped his face in her hands, touched and delighted that he thought so much of her—of her needs—to offer a compromise. "I'm not going to commute. I'm staying here, with you."

He frowned and she saw the confusion and the uncertainty in his eyes. "Sweetheart—" he took her hands in his, then pressed his lips to her palms "—as much as I want you here with me, all the time, I know how important Elijah Jane is to you. I can't let you give her up."

"I'm not giving her up, Sam. Digger and I are going to set up an office in Cactus Flat. The computer world is an amazing thing. We'll be able to run a new division right here in Cactus Flat, maybe open a couple of new restaurants in West Texas and New Mexico. I figure if Digger—my father—could do it for all those years, then so can I. Besides, I want our children to be close to Grandma and Grandpa."

"So Digger already knows about this, does he? I don't suppose he had anything to do with getting me in here to sign a marriage certificate, did he?"

"Well—" she said, her lips curving mischievously "—let's just say that we did agree that occasionally a little...strategy is necessary to ensure the success of a project."

He moved his lips over hers. "So I'm a project now, am I? So tell me, Madam President, will you be handling this project personally?"

She laughed softly against his mouth. "Every phase, with top priority, Mr. McCants."

She moved into the kiss, drew it out, then reluctantly pulled her lips from his. "By the way, I heard from my mother that Matilda came into an inheritance from a distant cousin. Quite a sum of money, I understand. More than enough for her husband to see that specialist in Dallas and take care of whatever bills they might have."

Sam smiled. "Digger Jones is still just plain old Digger Jones here in Cactus Flat. Although, between raising from the dead and marrying a fancy woman from Boston, he's as close to a legend as a man can get."

The organist began to play *Here Comes the Bride.* Sam pulled Faith closer, whispered against her ear, "Marry me, Faith. For real this time. Only for me."

She pressed her lips to his, smiled and replied softly, "I thought you'd never ask, cowboy."

* * * * *

Themed
Collections